THE MONSTER OF LAKE LOBO

Librarian Reviewer
Katharine Kan
Graphic novel reviewer and Library Consultant, Panama City, FL
MLS in Library and Information Studies, University of Hawaii at
Manoa, HI

Reading Consultant
Elizabeth Stedem
Educator/Consultant, Colorado Springs, CO
MA in Elementary Education, University of Denver, CO

STONE ARCH BOOKS
Minneapolis San Diego

Graphic Sparks are published by Stone Arch Books
151 Good Counsel Drive, P.O. Box 669
Mankato, Minnesota 56002
www.stonearchbooks.com

Copyright © 2008 by Stone Arch Books

Library of Congress Cataloging-in-Publication Data
Nickel, Scott.
    The Monster of Lake Lobo / by Scott Nickel; illustrated by Enrique Corts.
    p. cm. — (Graphic Sparks)
    ISBN-13: 978-1-59889-836-1 (library binding)
    ISBN-10: 1-59889-836-1 (library binding)
    ISBN-13: 978-1-59889-892-7 (paperback)
    ISBN-10: 1-59889-892-2 (paperback)
    1. Graphic novels. I. Corts, Enrique. II. Title.
PN6727.N544M66 2008
741.5'973—dc22   2007003178

Summary: When Kevin and his dad visit Lake Lobo, their summer vacation suddenly
turns creepy. Who made the claw marks outside their cabin window? What is howling in
the night? Local legends say a strange creature prowls the woods. Could Kevin's new dog
hold the secret to the monster of Lake Lobo?

Art Director: Heather Kindseth
Graphic Designer: Brann Garvey

1 2 3 4 5 6 12 11 10 09 08 07

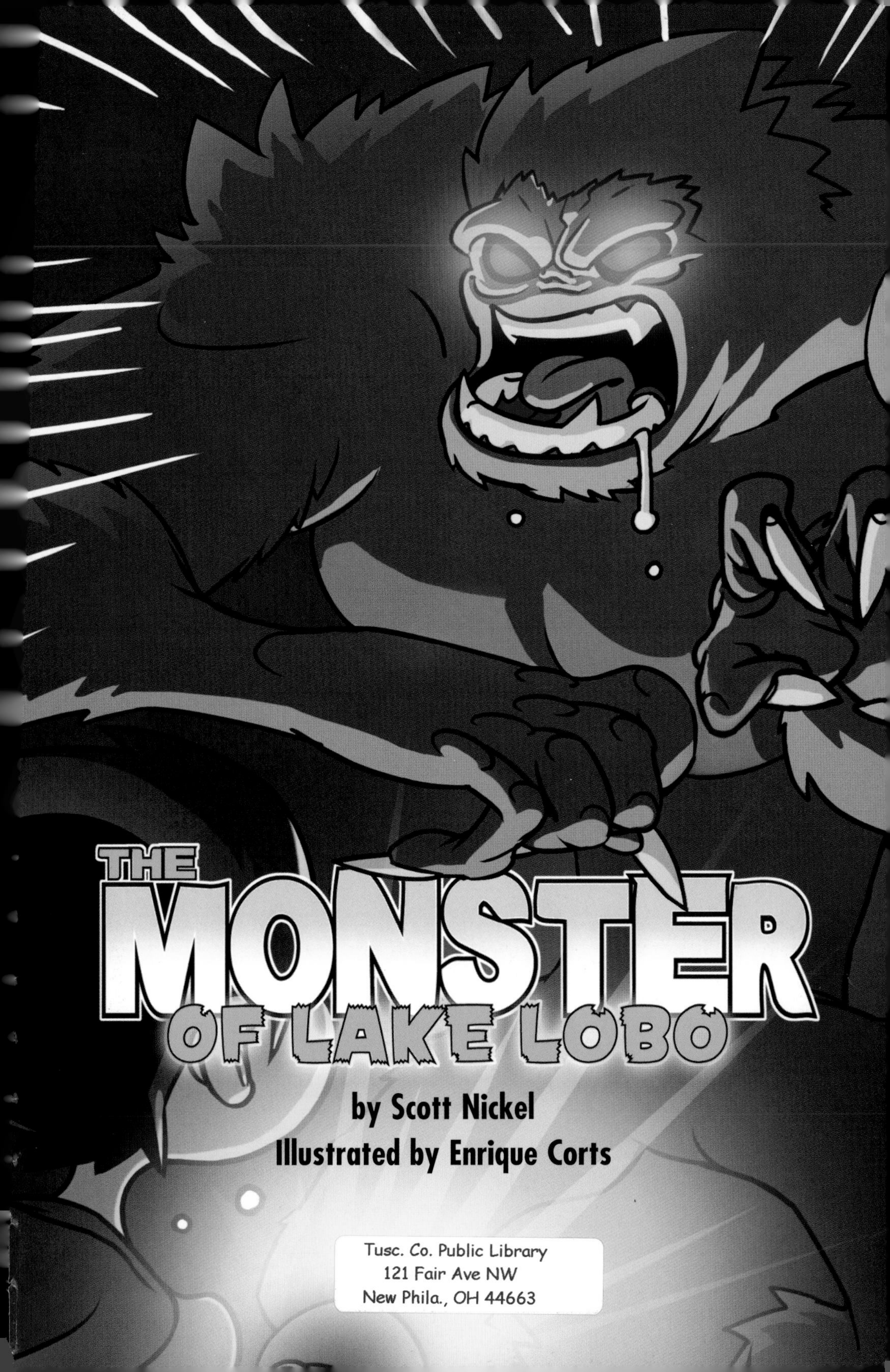

THE MONSTER OF LAKE LOBO

by Scott Nickel

Illustrated by Enrique Corts

CAST OF CHARACTERS

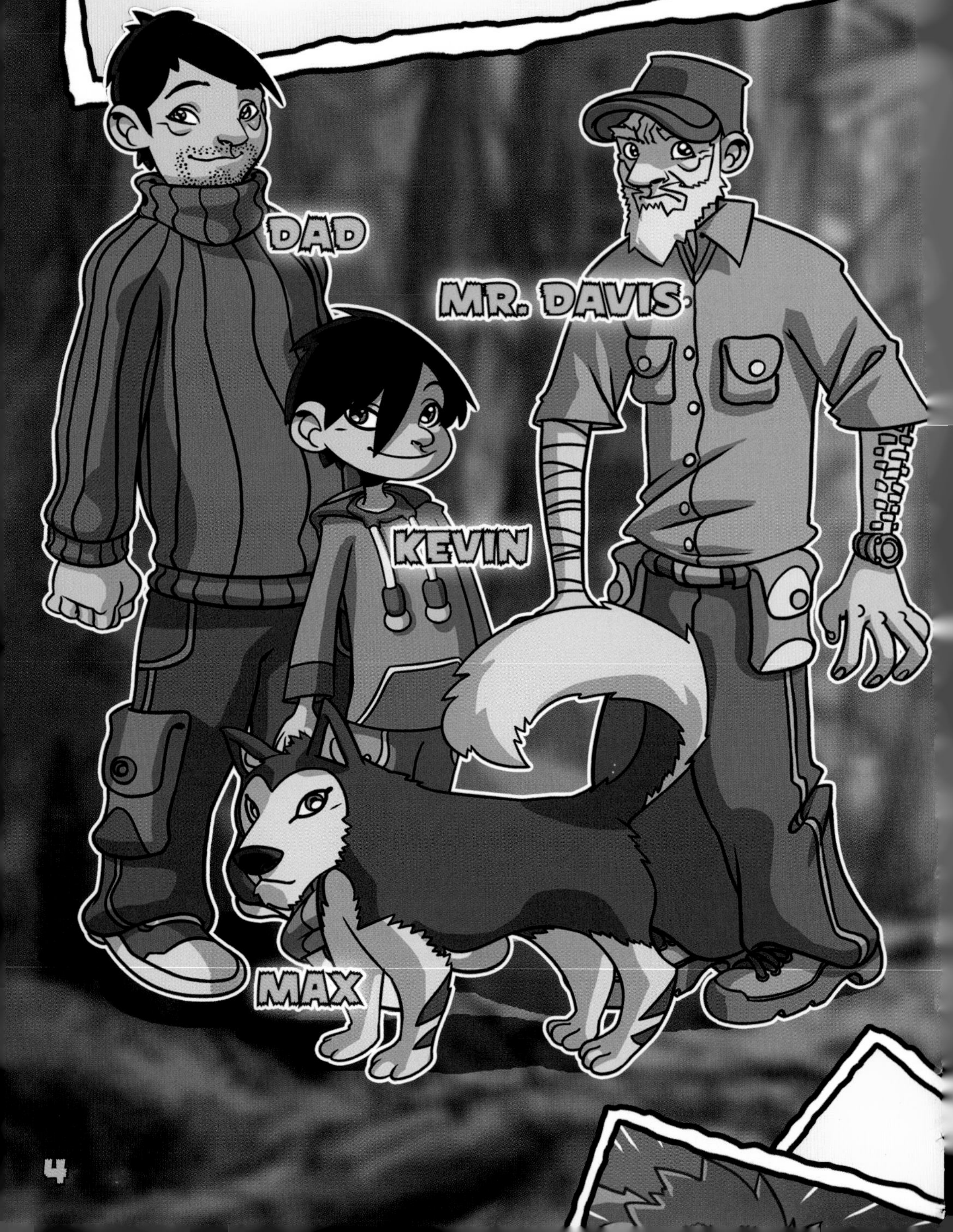
DAD
MR. DAVIS
KEVIN
MAX

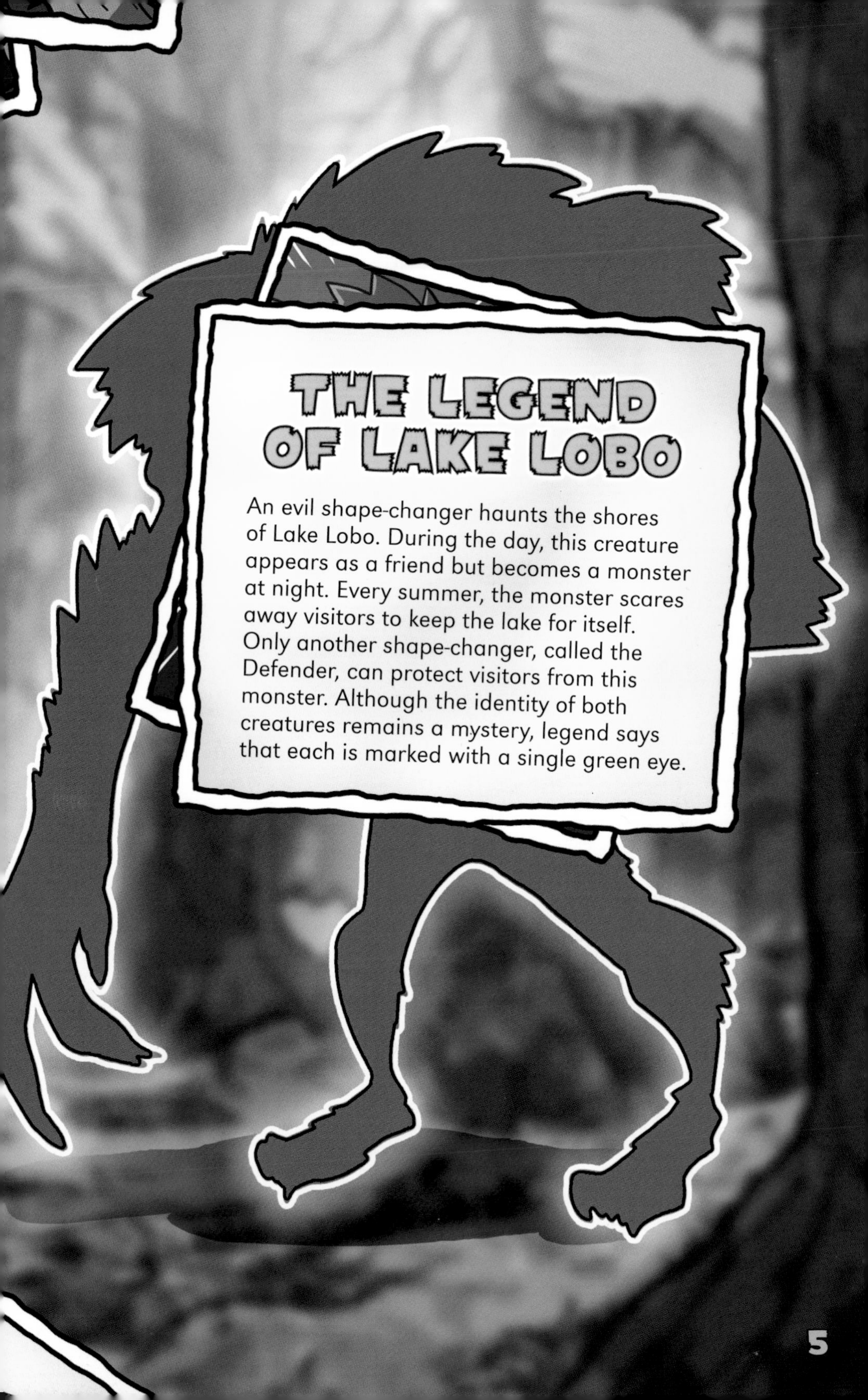

THE LEGEND OF LAKE LOBO

An evil shape-changer haunts the shores of Lake Lobo. During the day, this creature appears as a friend but becomes a monster at night. Every summer, the monster scares away visitors to keep the lake for itself. Only another shape-changer, called the Defender, can protect visitors from this monster. Although the identity of both creatures remains a mystery, legend says that each is marked with a single green eye.

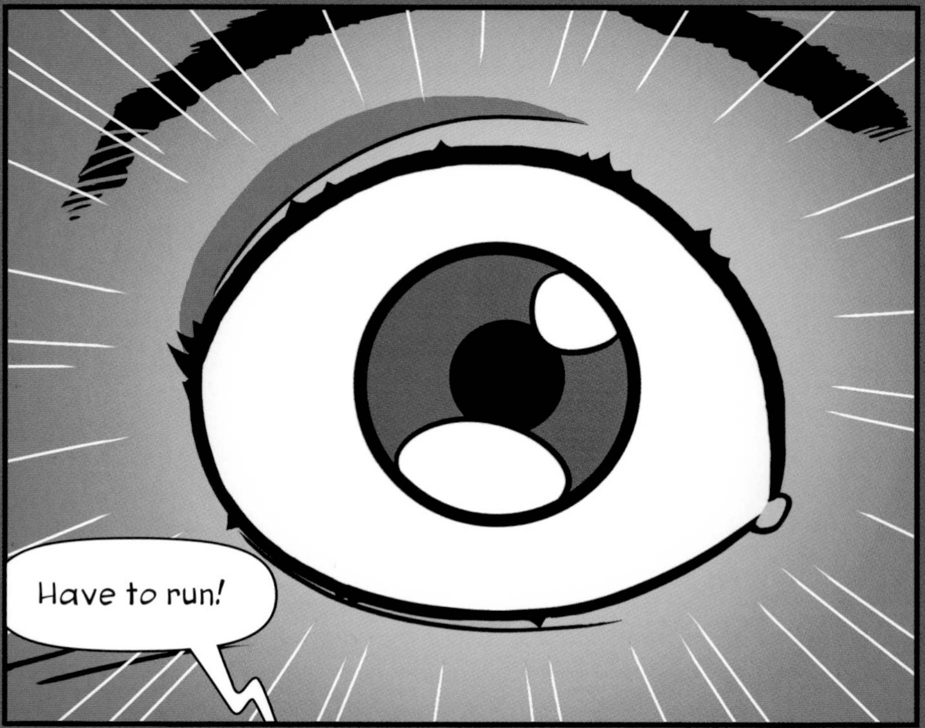
Have to run!

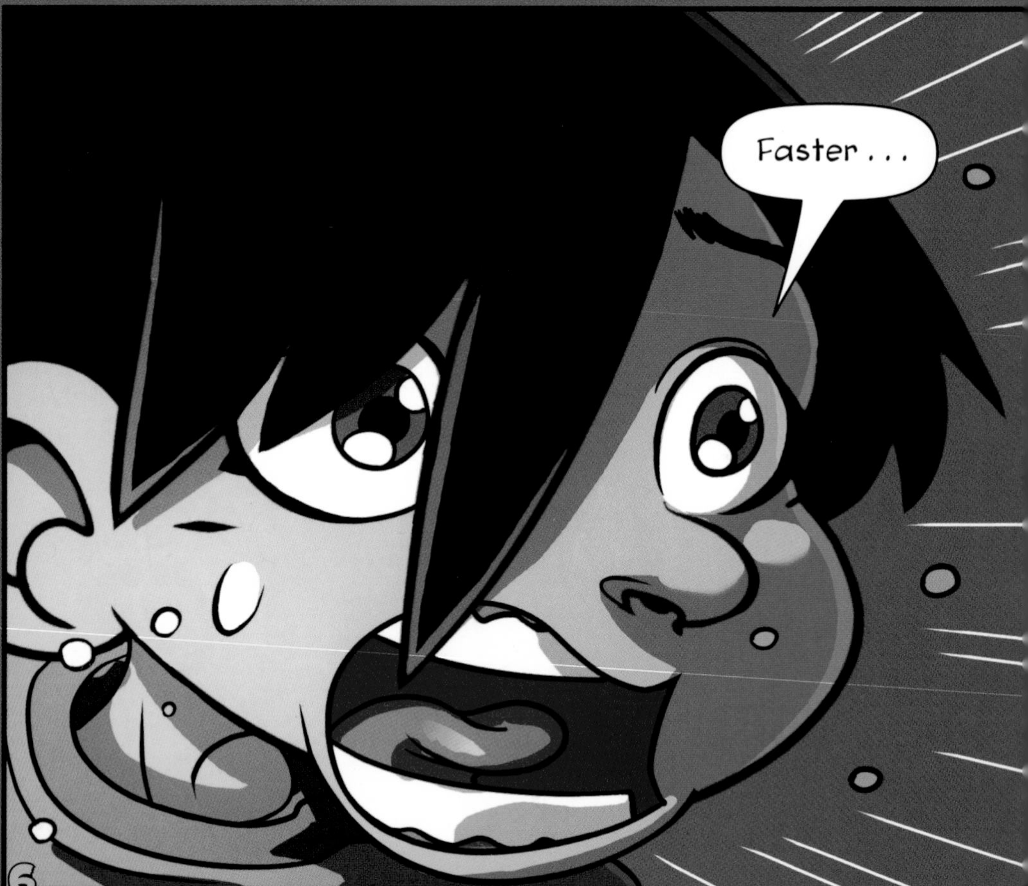
Faster . . .

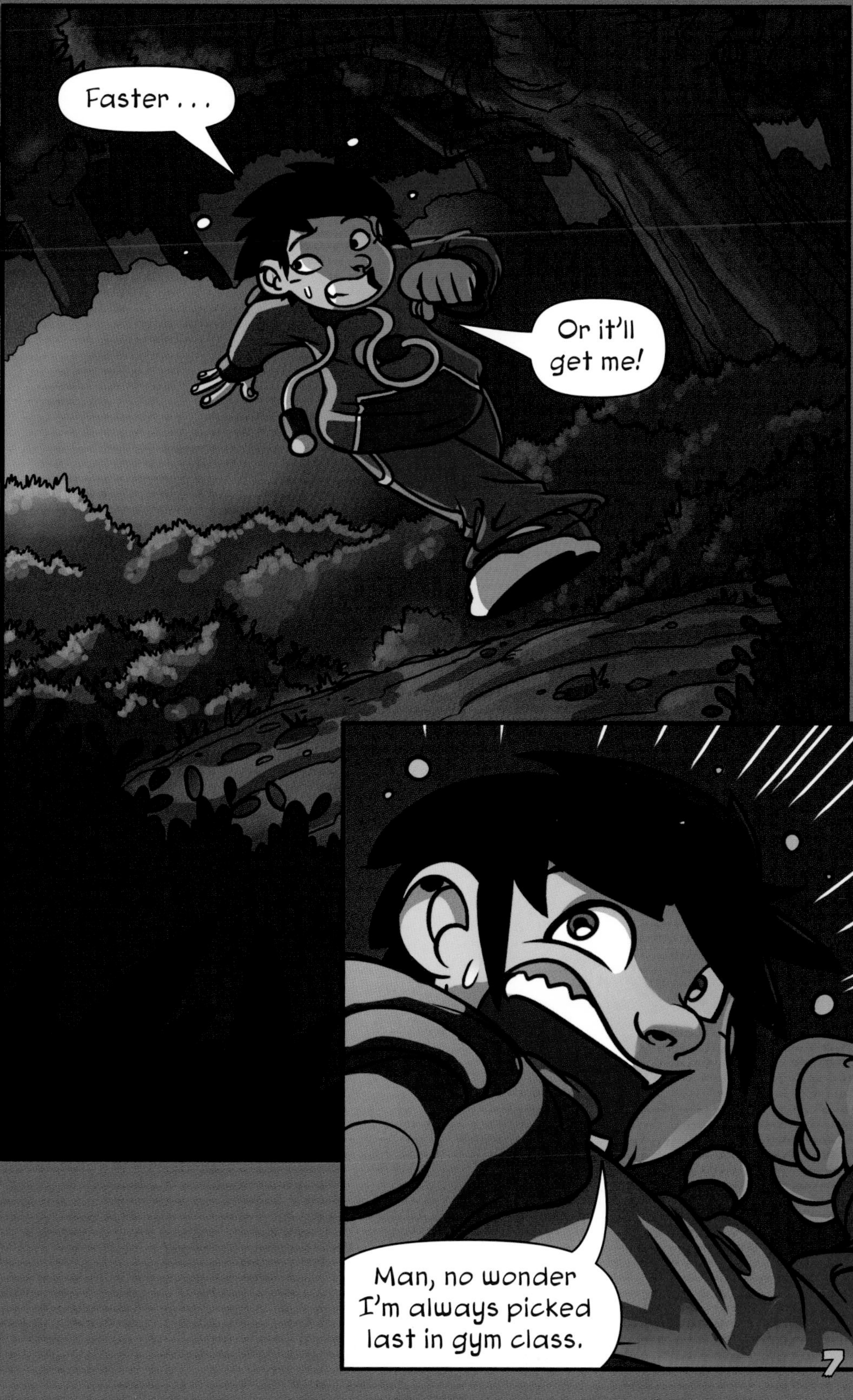
Faster . . .
Or it'll get me!
Man, no wonder I'm always picked last in gym class.

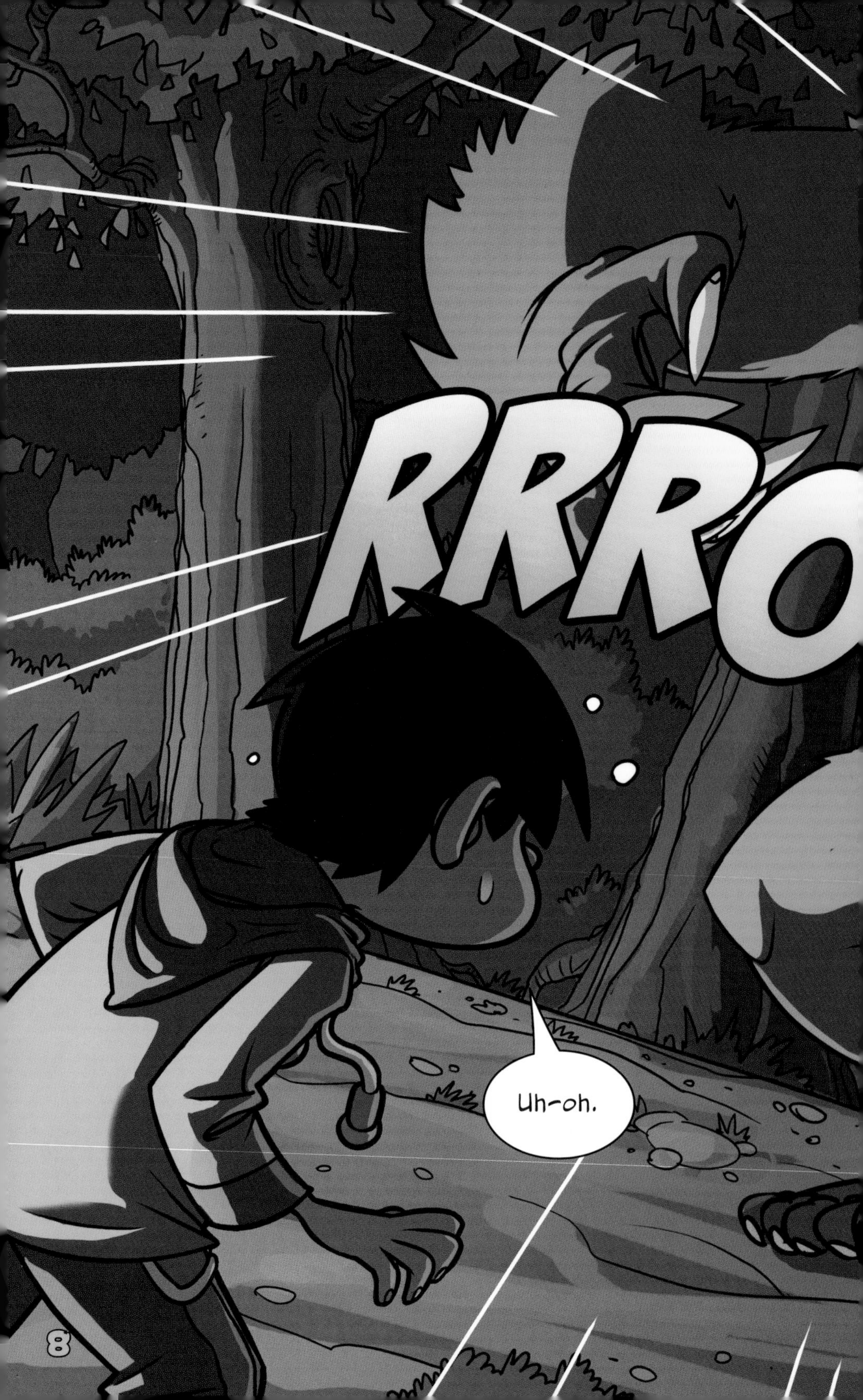
RRRO
Uh-oh.

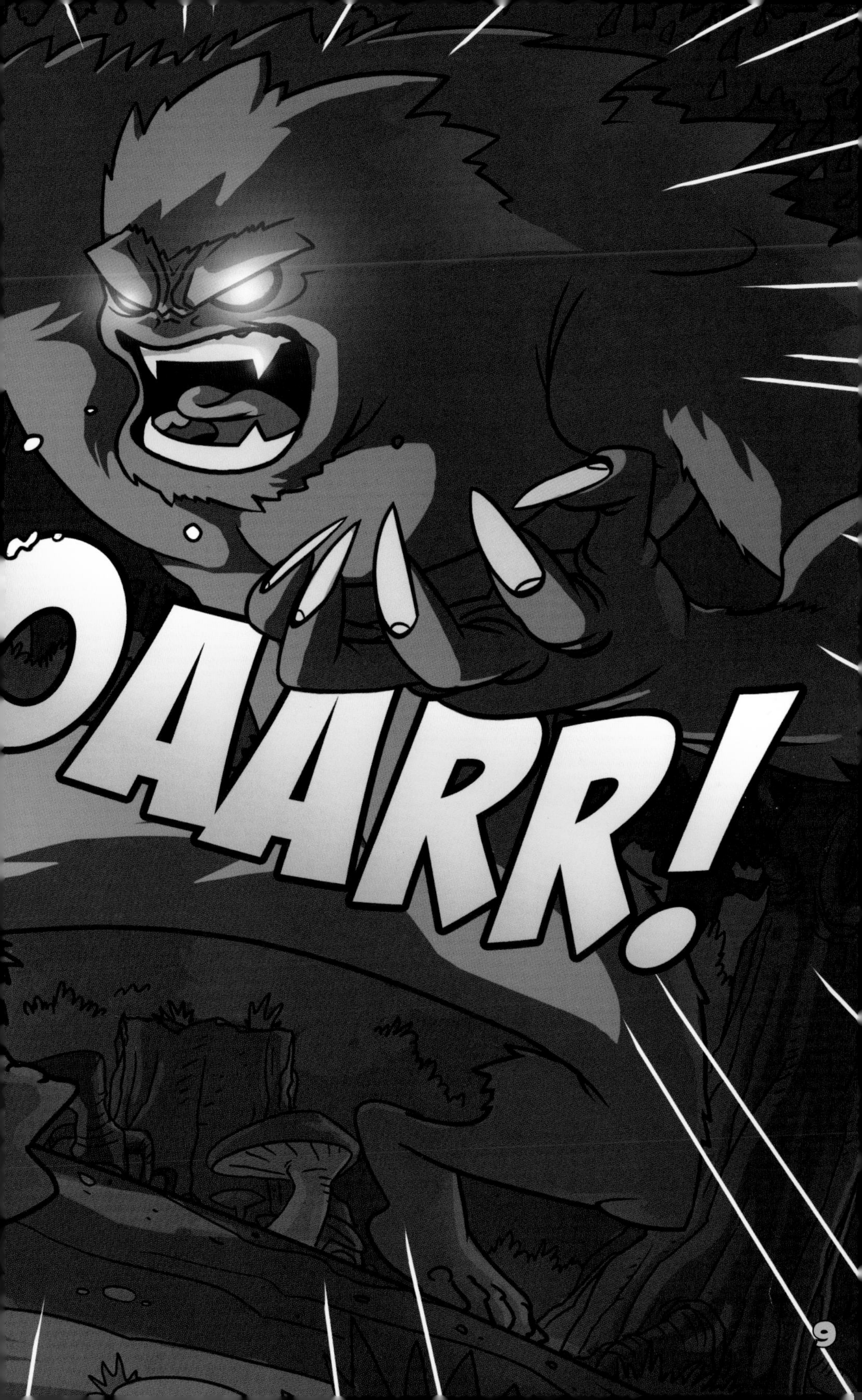
AARR!

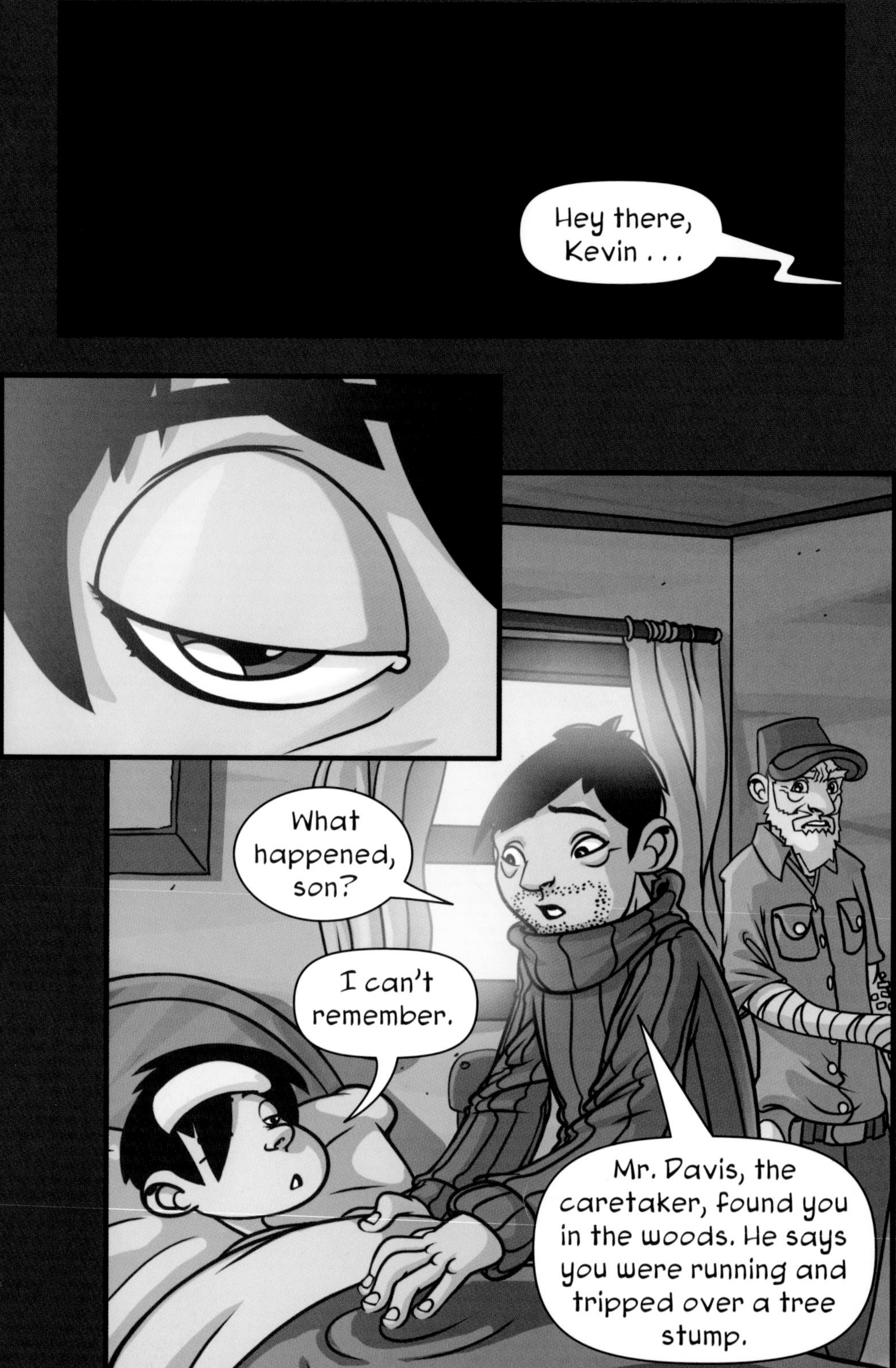
Hey there, Kevin . . .
What happened, son?
I can't remember.
Mr. Davis, the caretaker, found you in the woods. He says you were running and tripped over a tree stump.

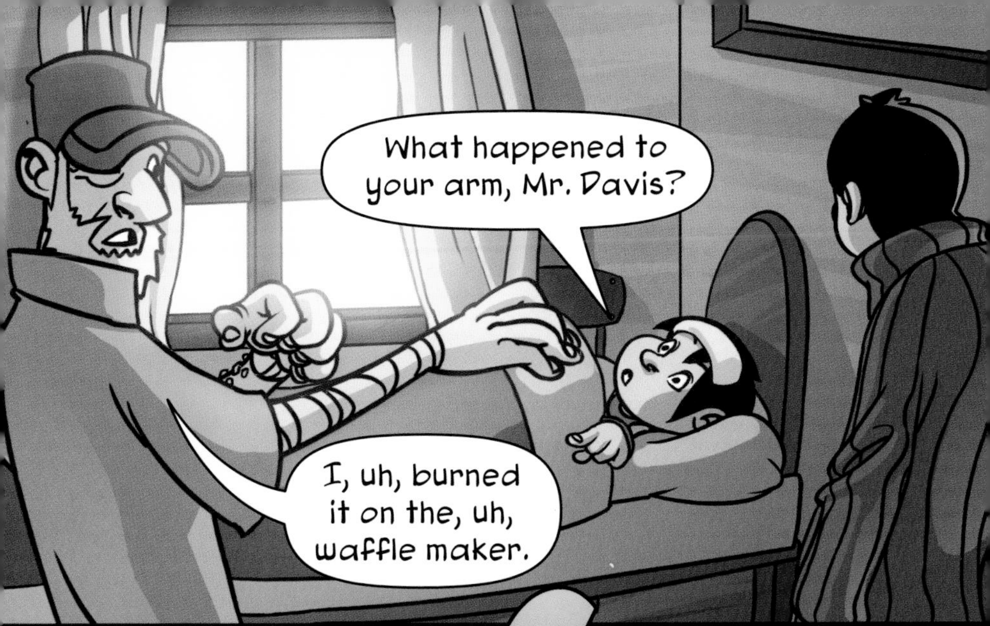
What happened to your arm, Mr. Davis?
I, uh, burned it on the, uh, waffle maker.

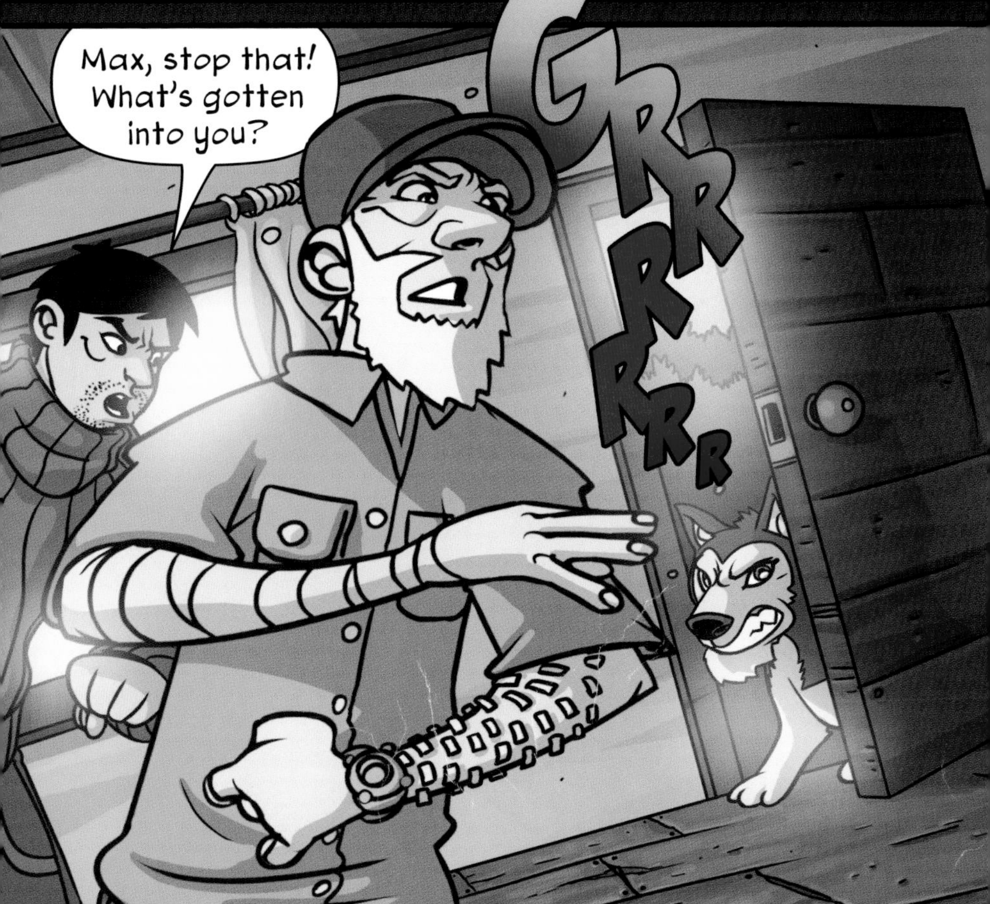
Max, stop that! What's gotten into you?
GRRRRRRR

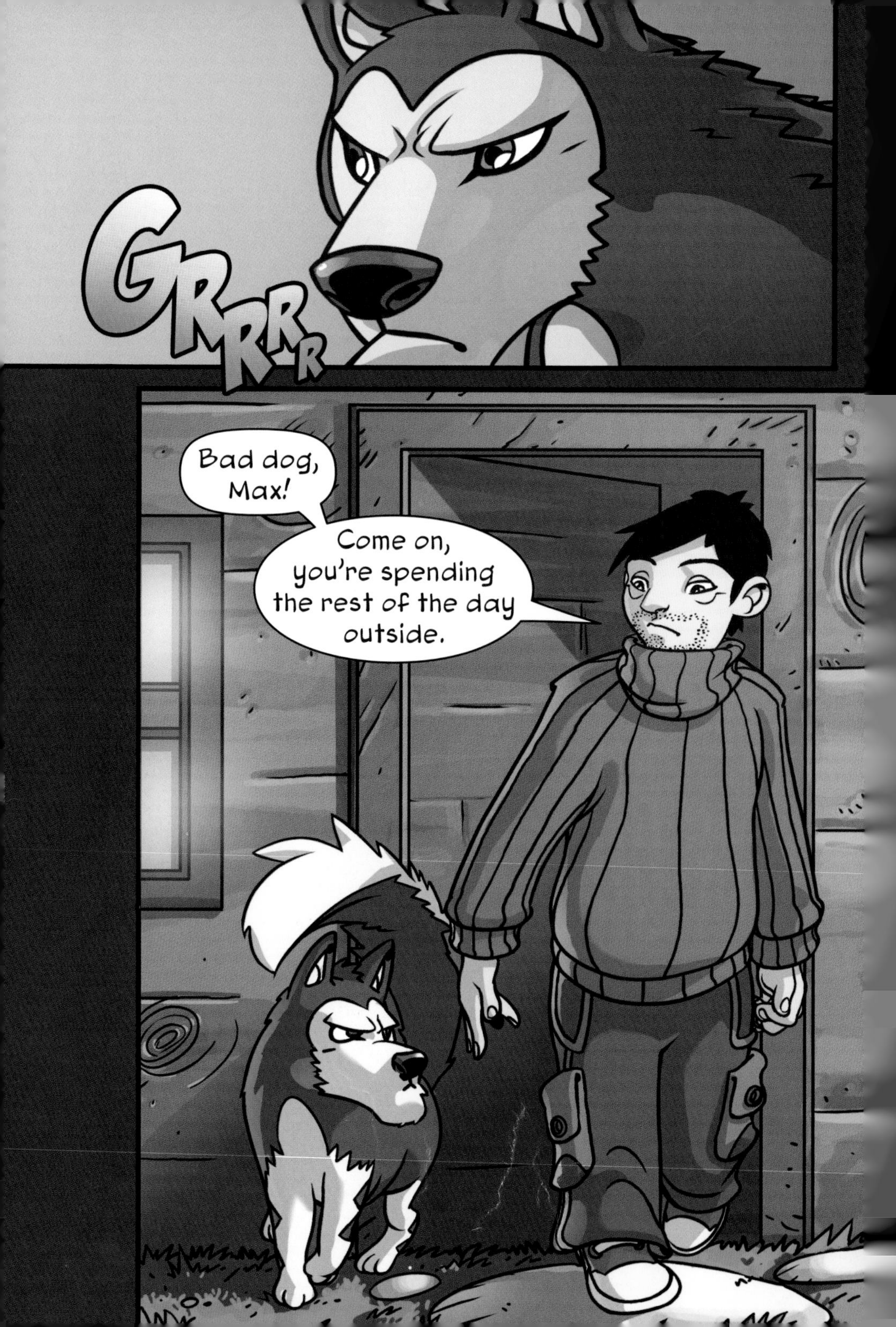
GRRRRR
Bad dog, Max!
Come on, you're spending the rest of the day outside.

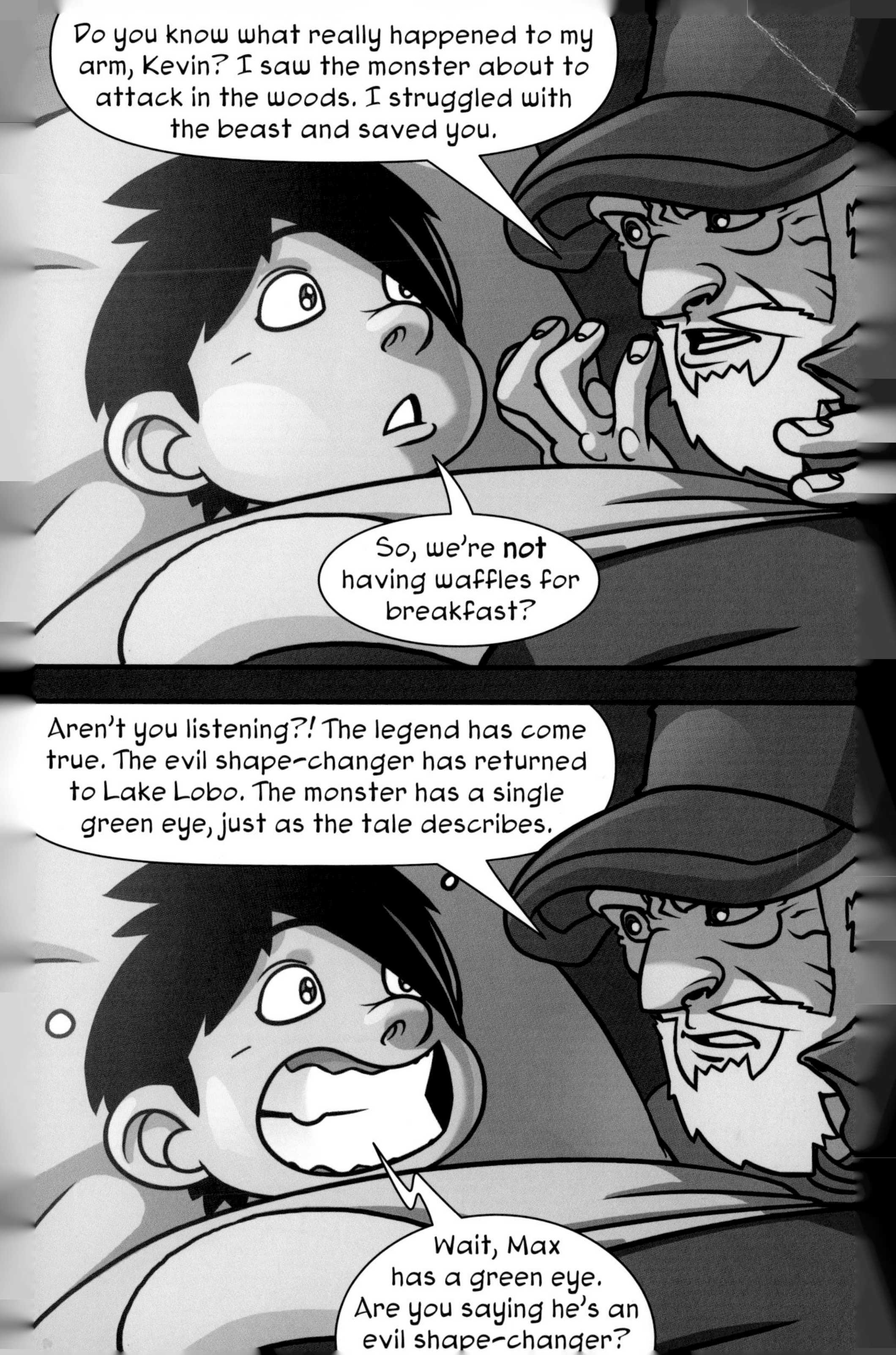

Do you know what really happened to my arm, Kevin? I saw the monster about to attack in the woods. I struggled with the beast and saved you.
So, we're **not** having waffles for breakfast?
Aren't you listening?! The legend has come true. The evil shape-changer has returned to Lake Lobo. The monster has a single green eye, just as the tale describes.
Wait, Max has a green eye. Are you saying he's an evil shape-changer?

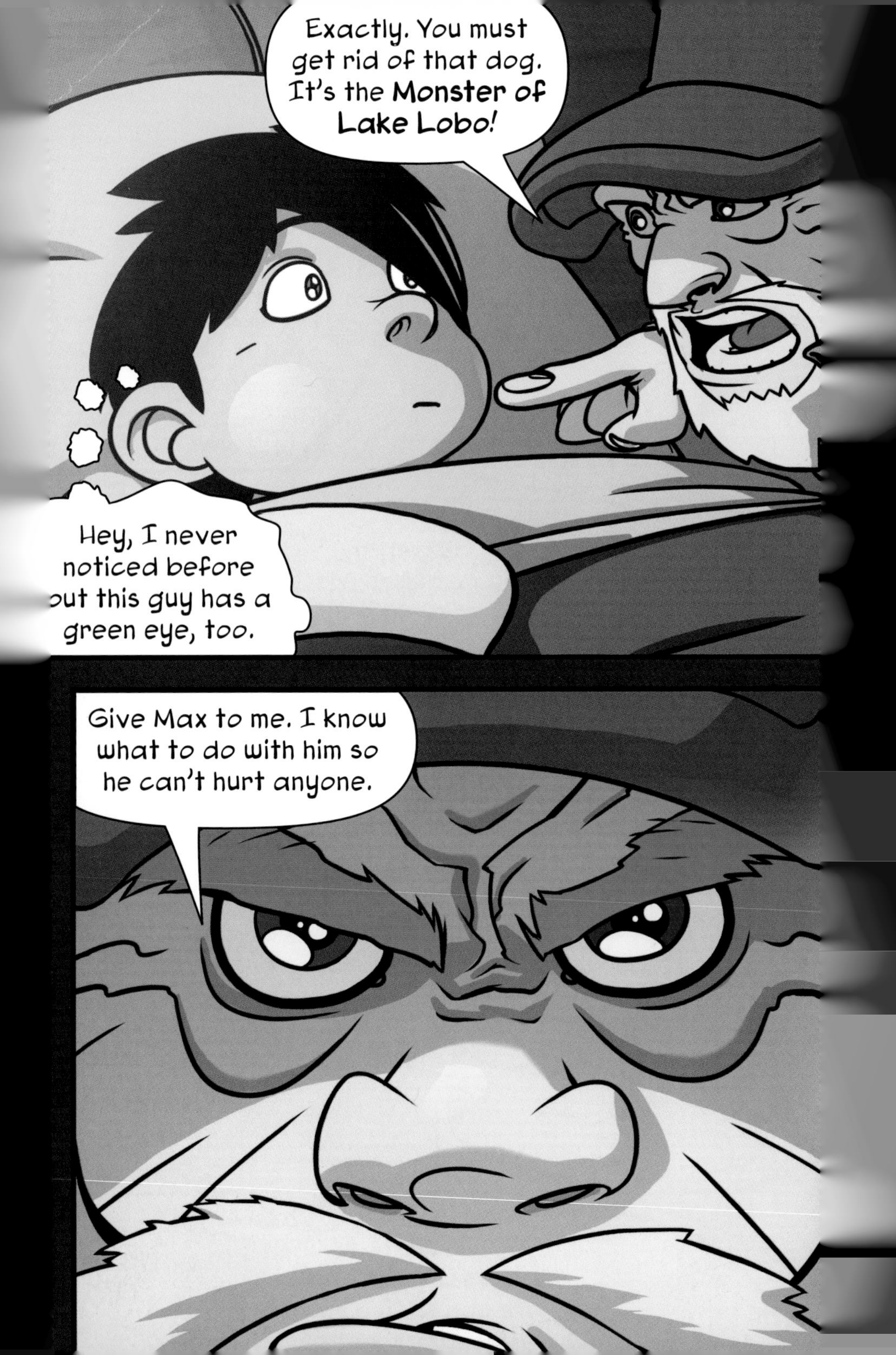
Exactly. You must get rid of that dog. It's the **Monster of Lake Lobo!**
Hey, I never noticed before out this guy has a green eye, too.
Give Max to me. I know what to do with him so he can't hurt anyone.

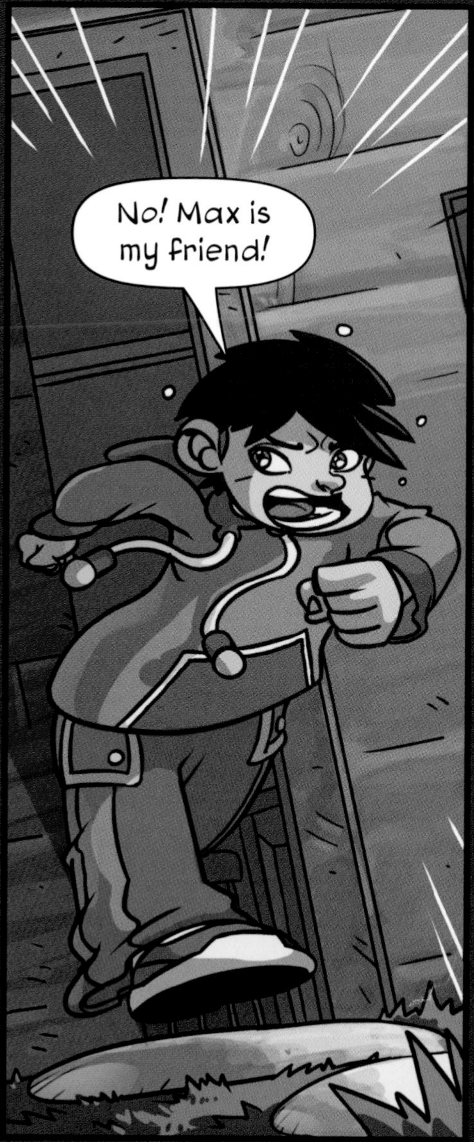
No! Max is my friend!

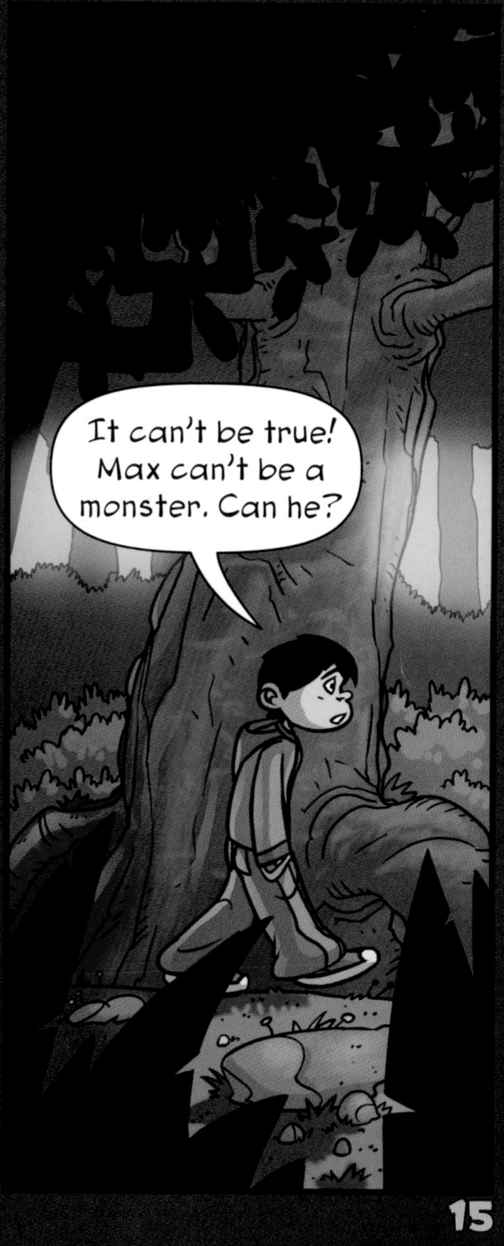
It can't be true! Max can't be a monster. Can he?

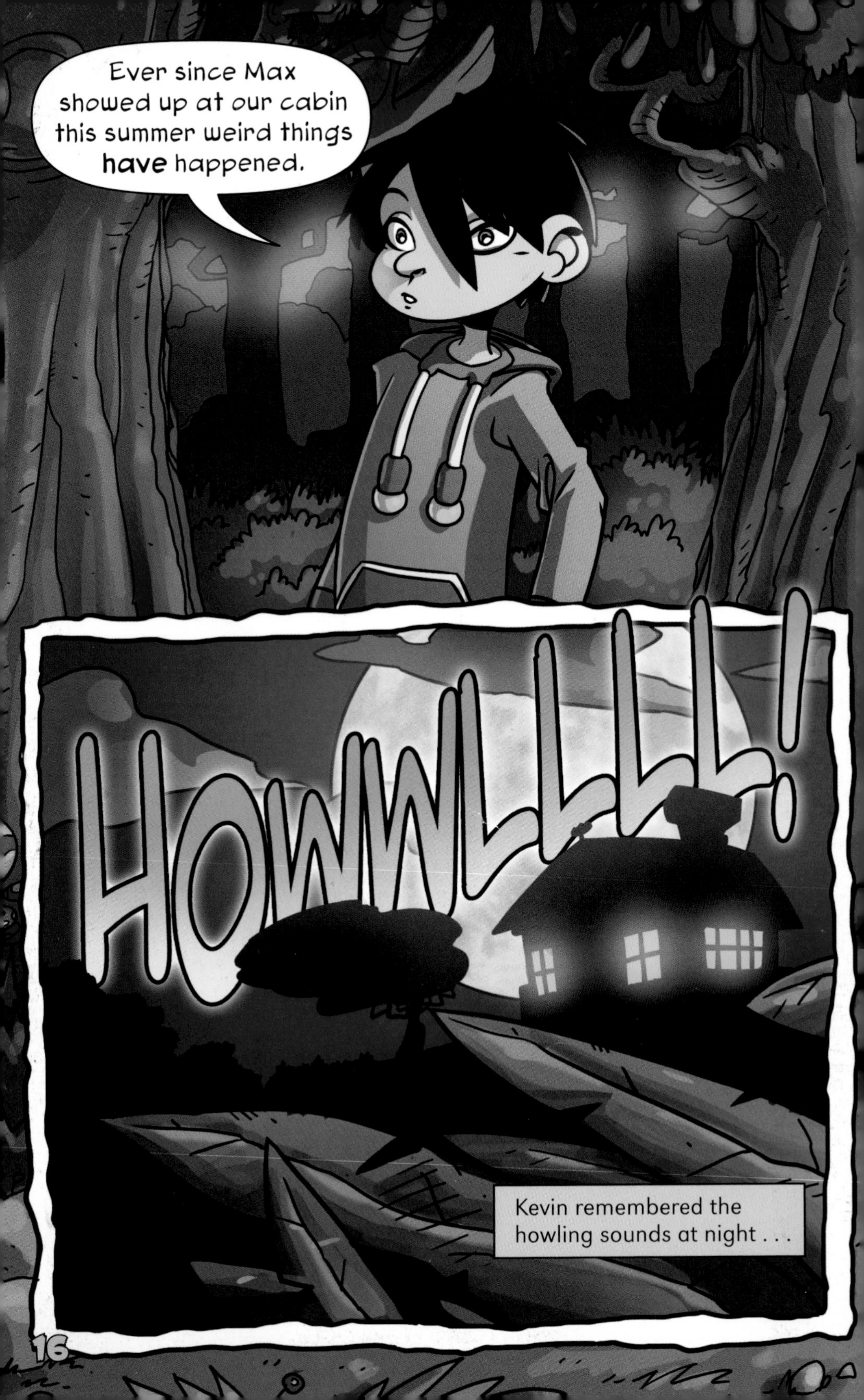
Ever since Max showed up at our cabin this summer weird things **have** happened.
HOWLLLL!
Kevin remembered the howling sounds at night . . .

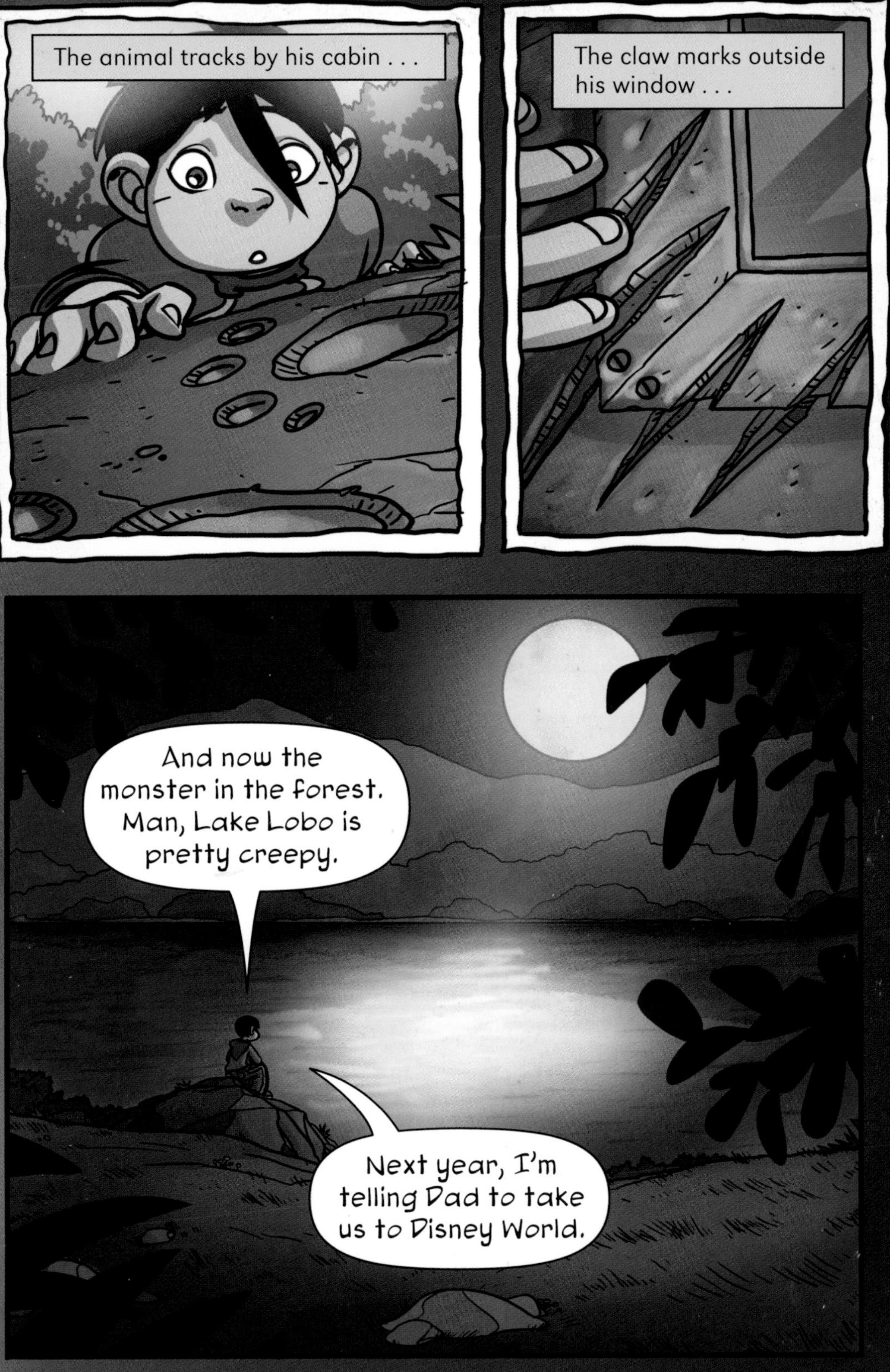

The animal tracks by his cabin . . .
The claw marks outside his window . . .
And now the monster in the forest. Man, Lake Lobo is pretty creepy.
Next year, I'm telling Dad to take us to Disney World.

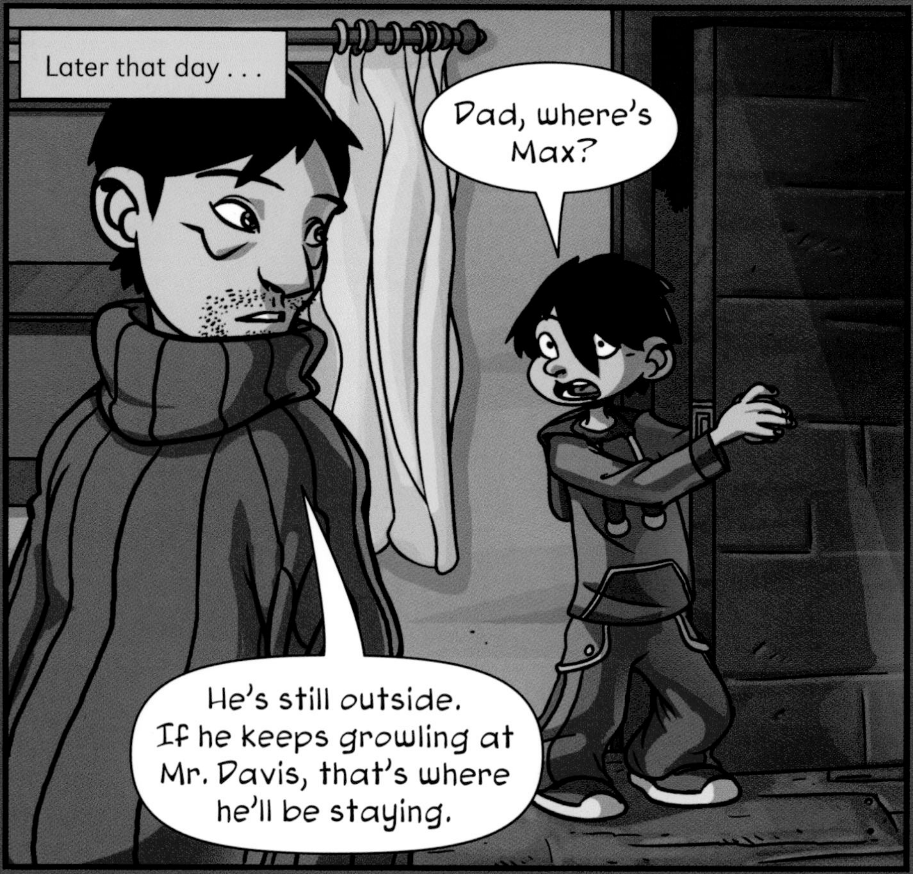
Later that day . . .
Dad, where's Max?
He's still outside. If he keeps growling at Mr. Davis, that's where he'll be staying.

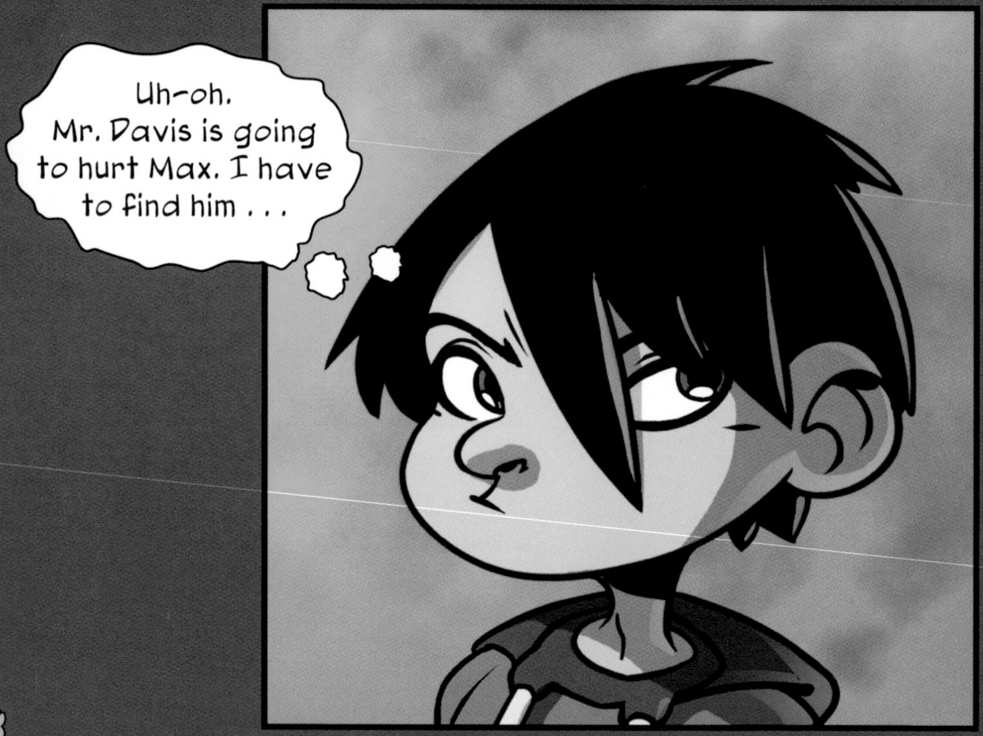
Uh-oh. Mr. Davis is going to hurt Max. I have to find him . . .

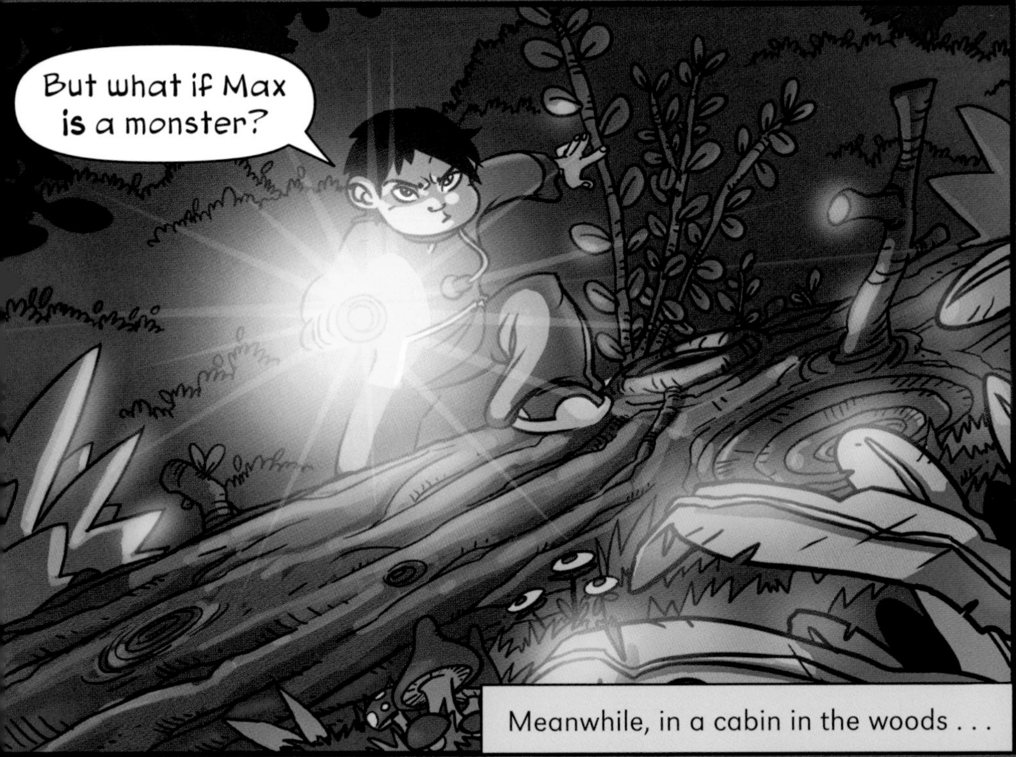
But what if Max **is** a monster?
Meanwhile, in a cabin in the woods . . .

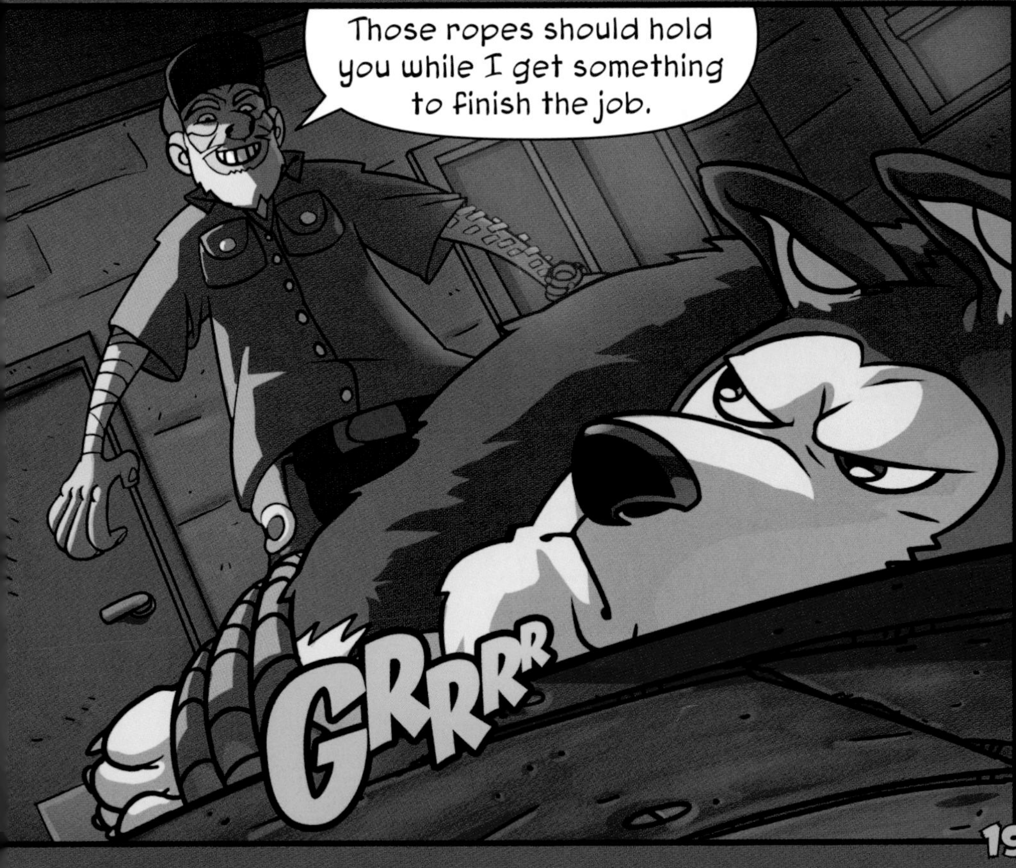
Those ropes should hold you while I get something to finish the job.
GRRRR

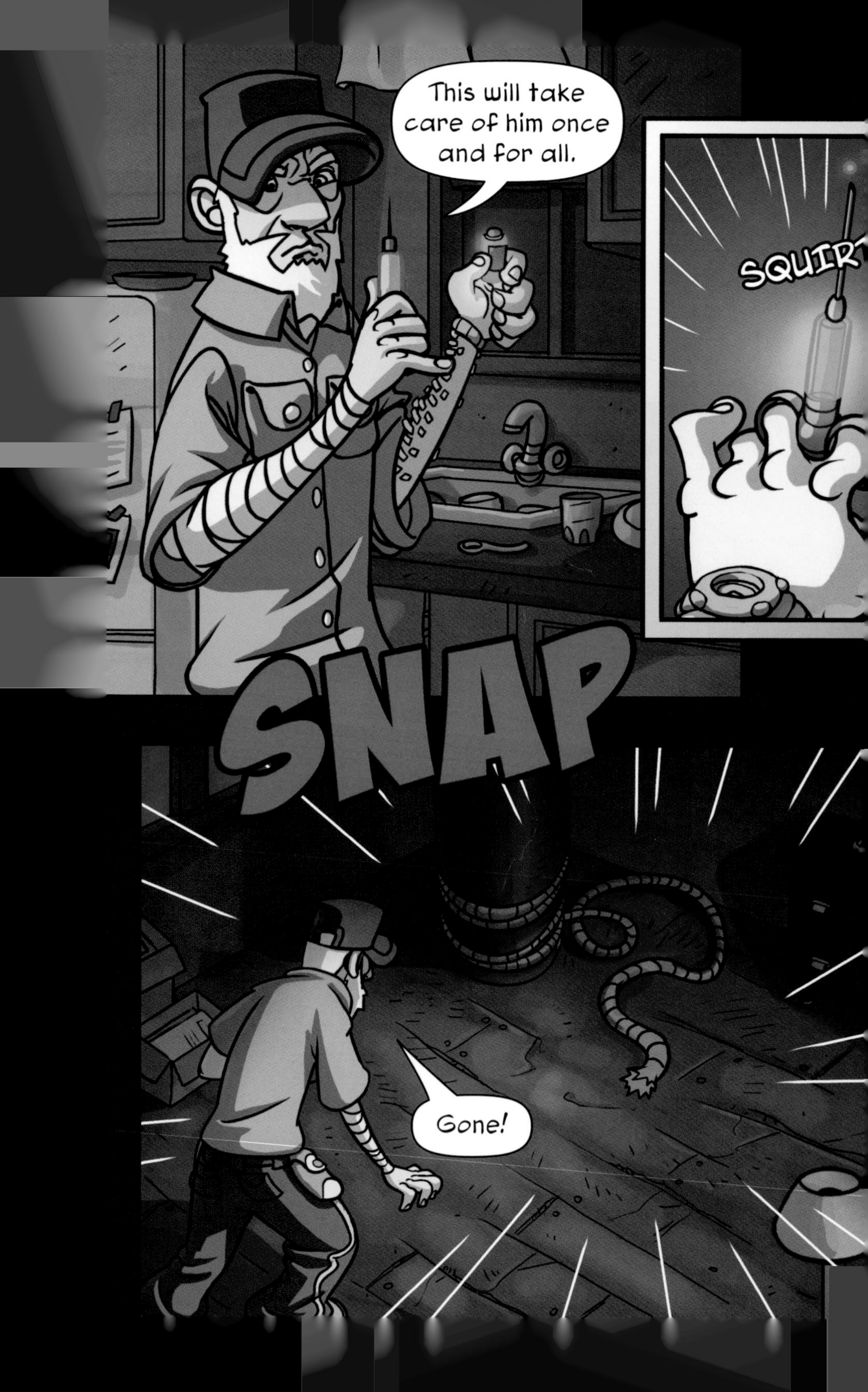
This will take care of him once and for all.
SQUIRT
SNAP
Gone!

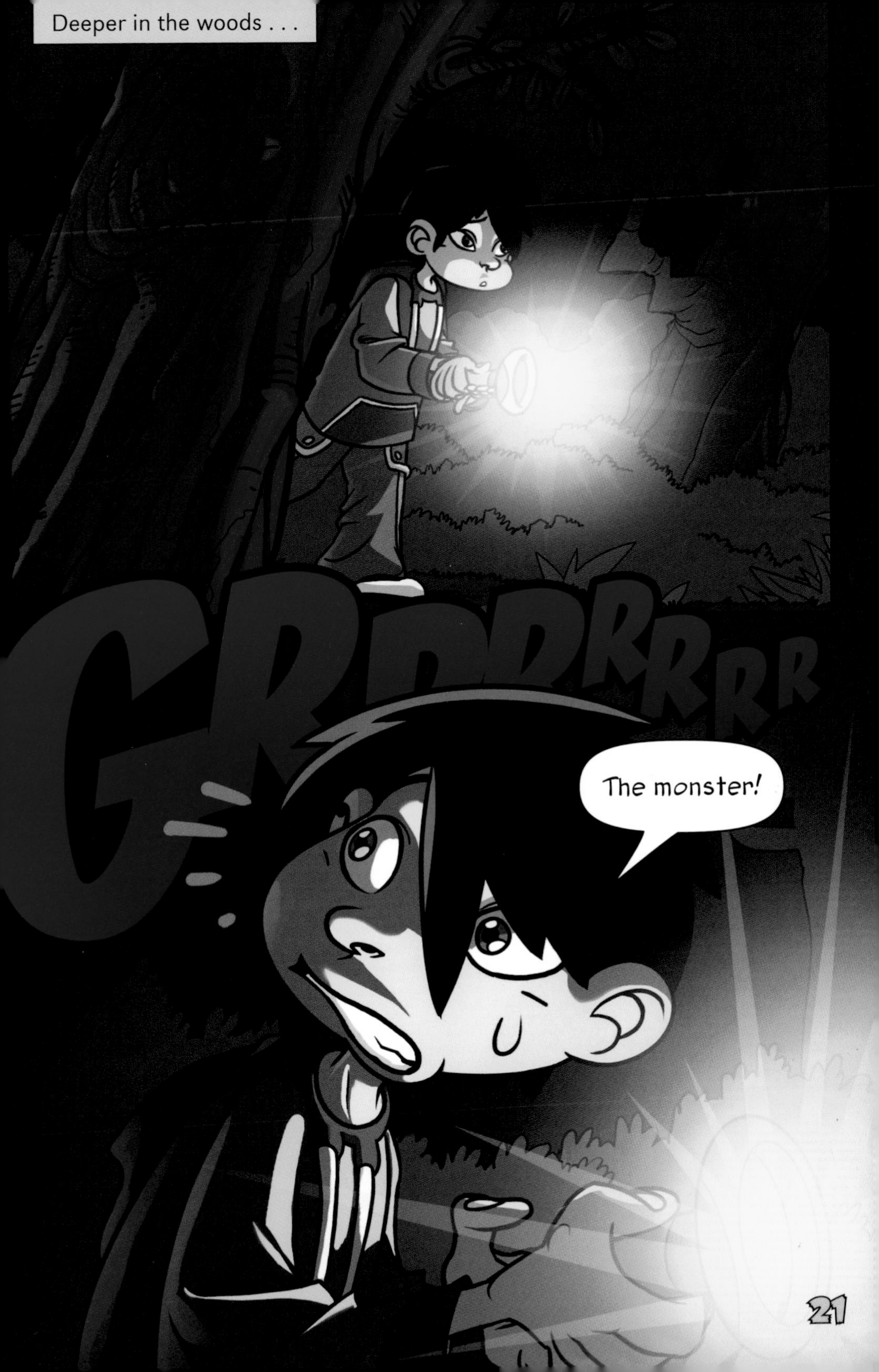
Deeper in the woods . . .
GRRRRRRR
The monster!

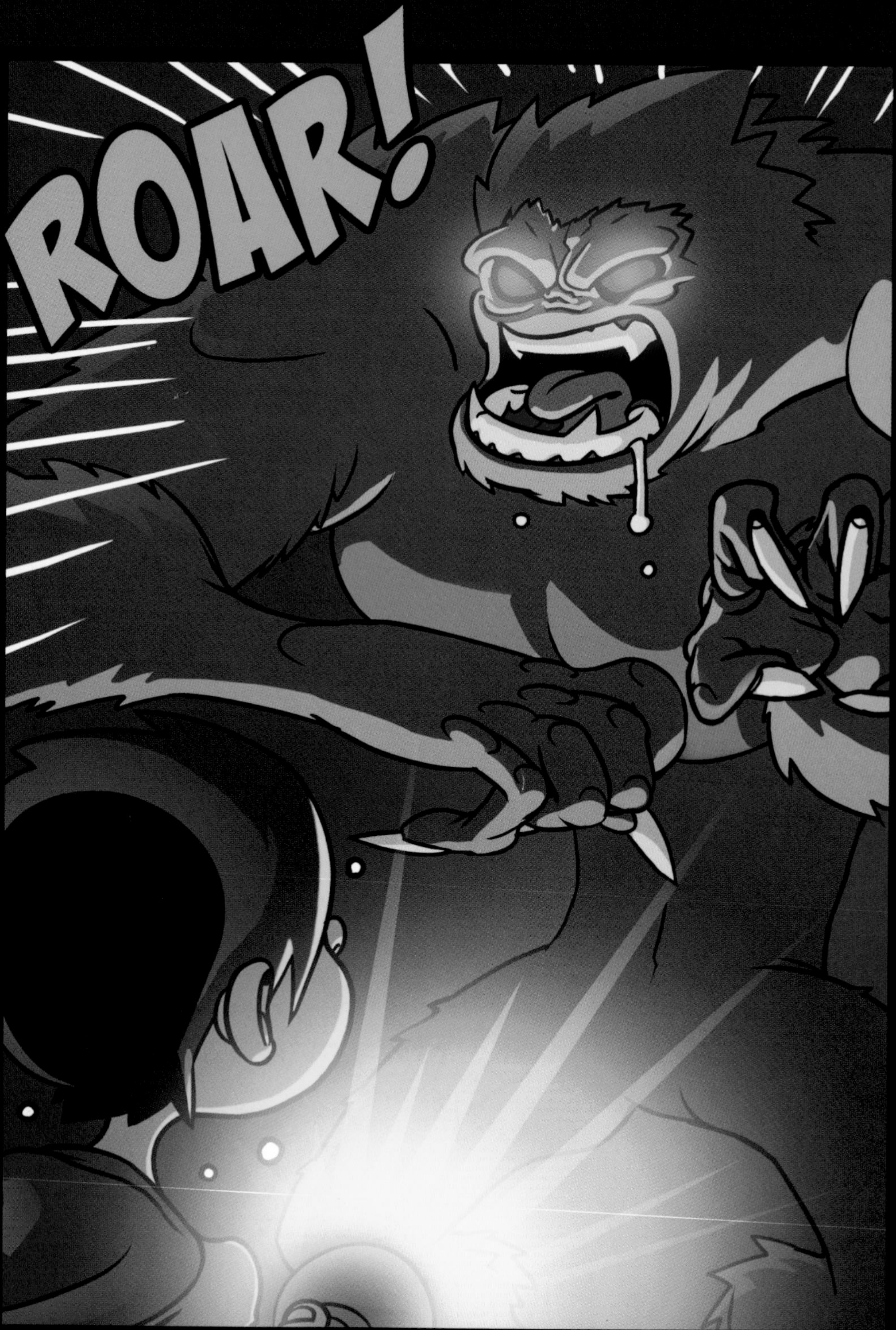
ROAR!

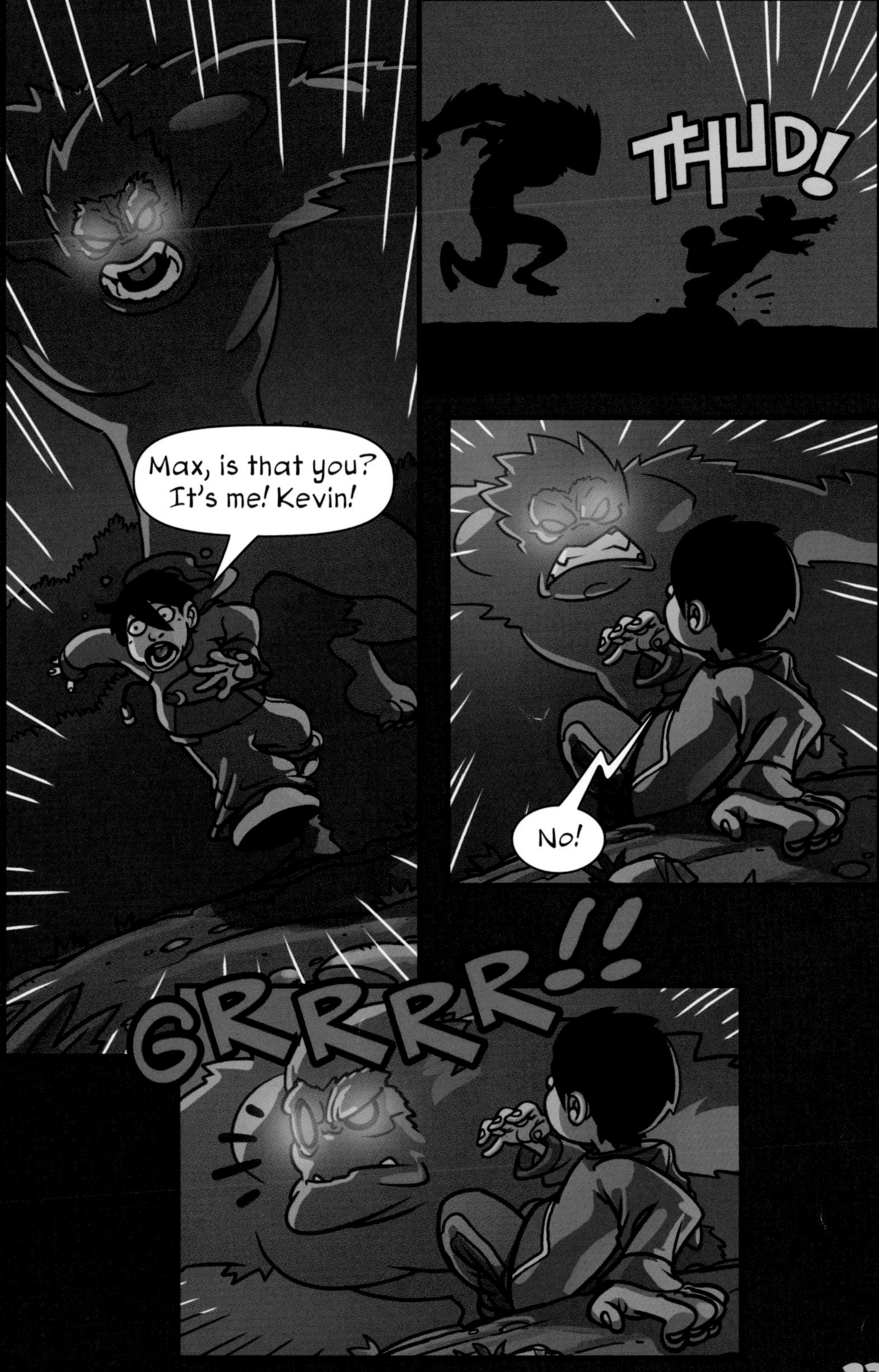
THUD!
Max, is that you? It's me! Kevin!
No!
GRRRR!!

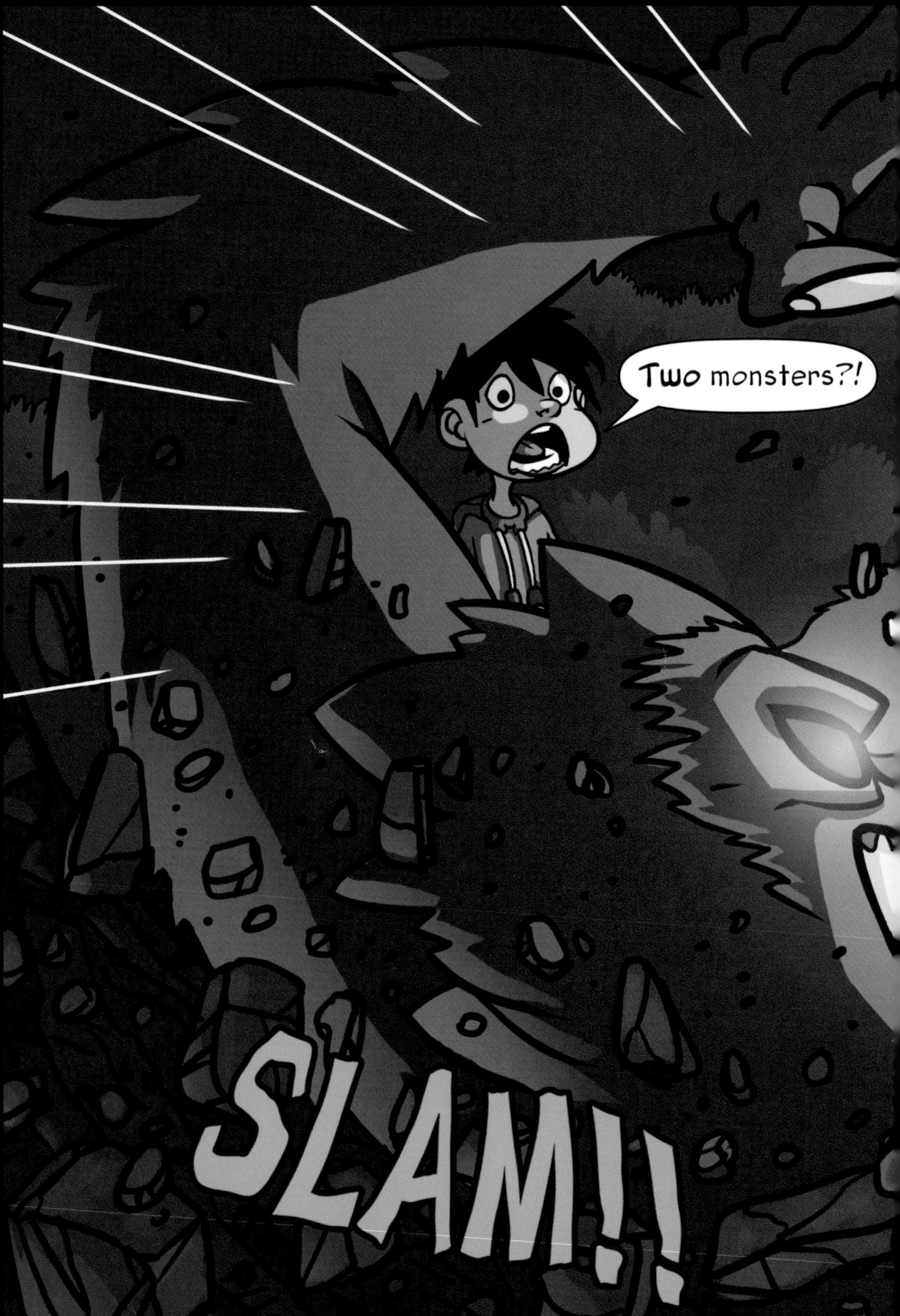
Two monsters?!
SLAM!!

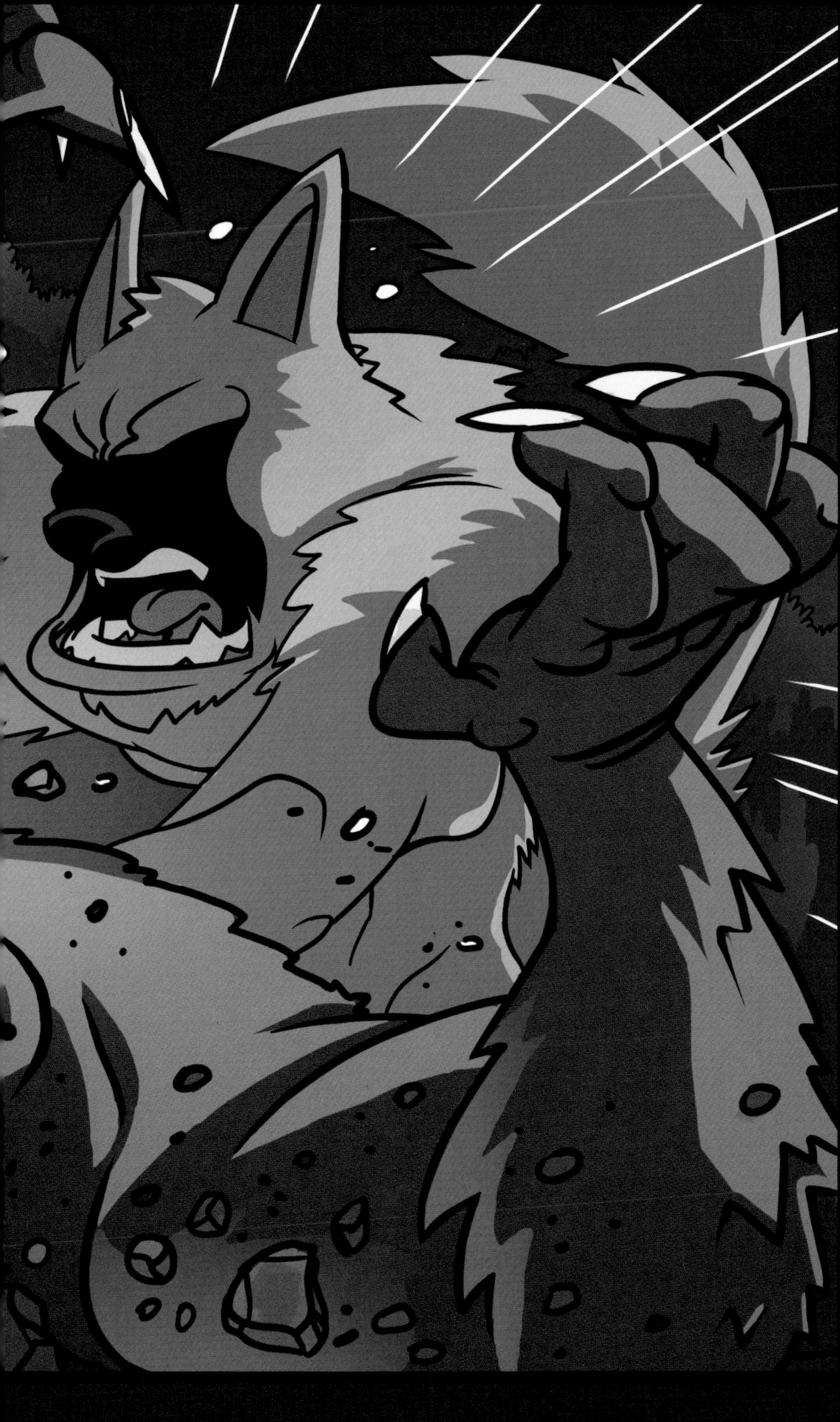

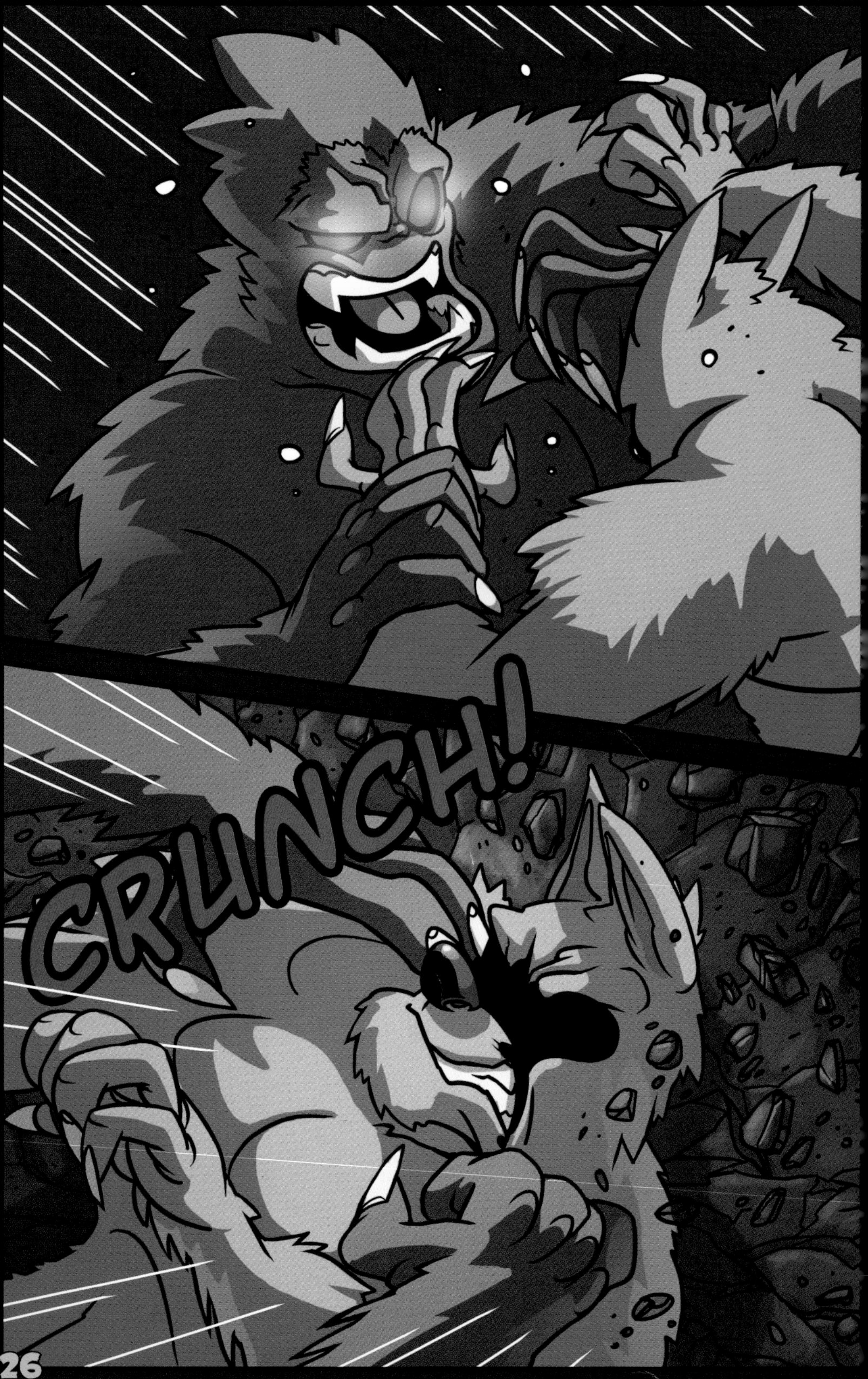
CRUNCH!

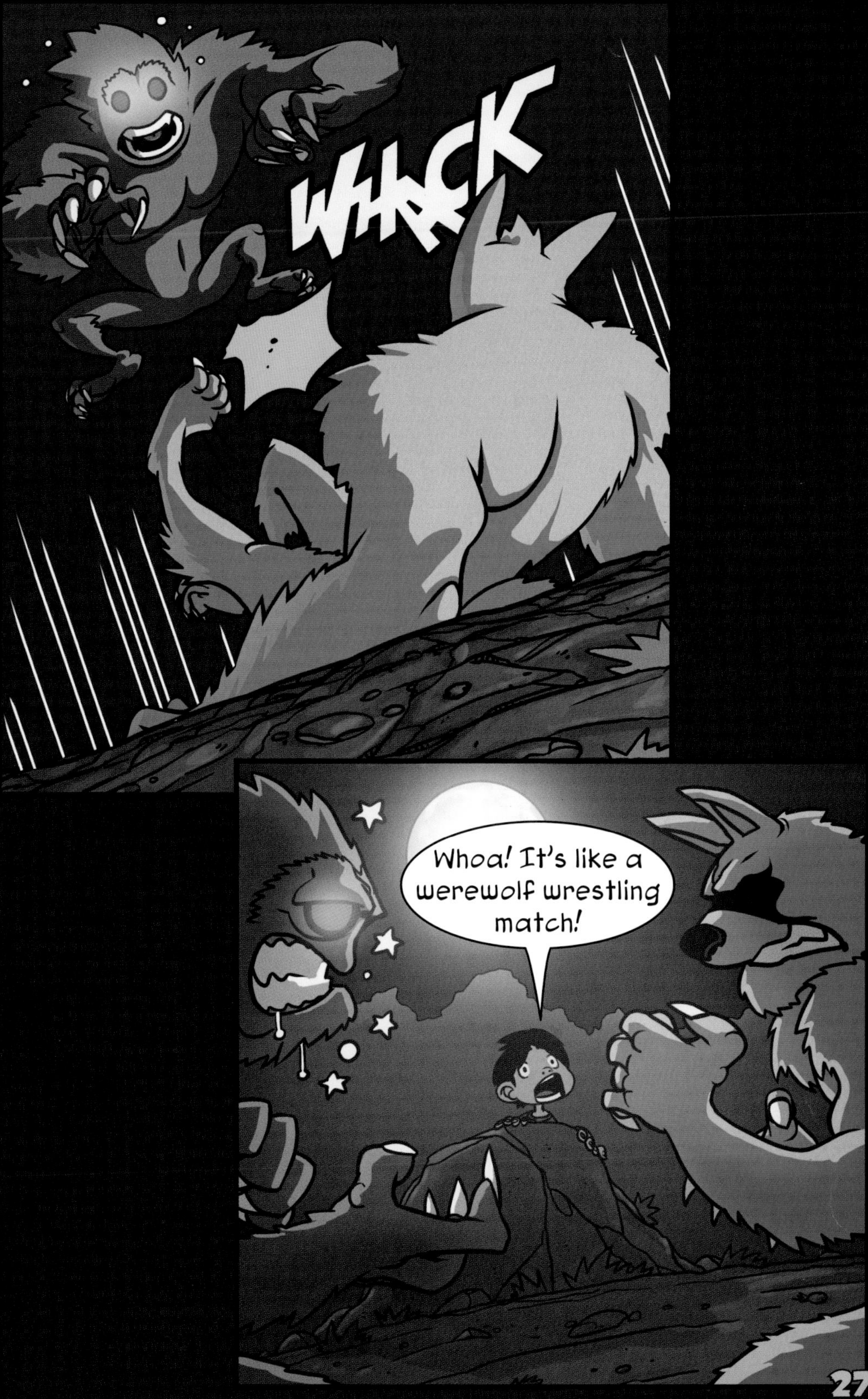
WHACK
Whoa! It's like a werewolf wrestling match!

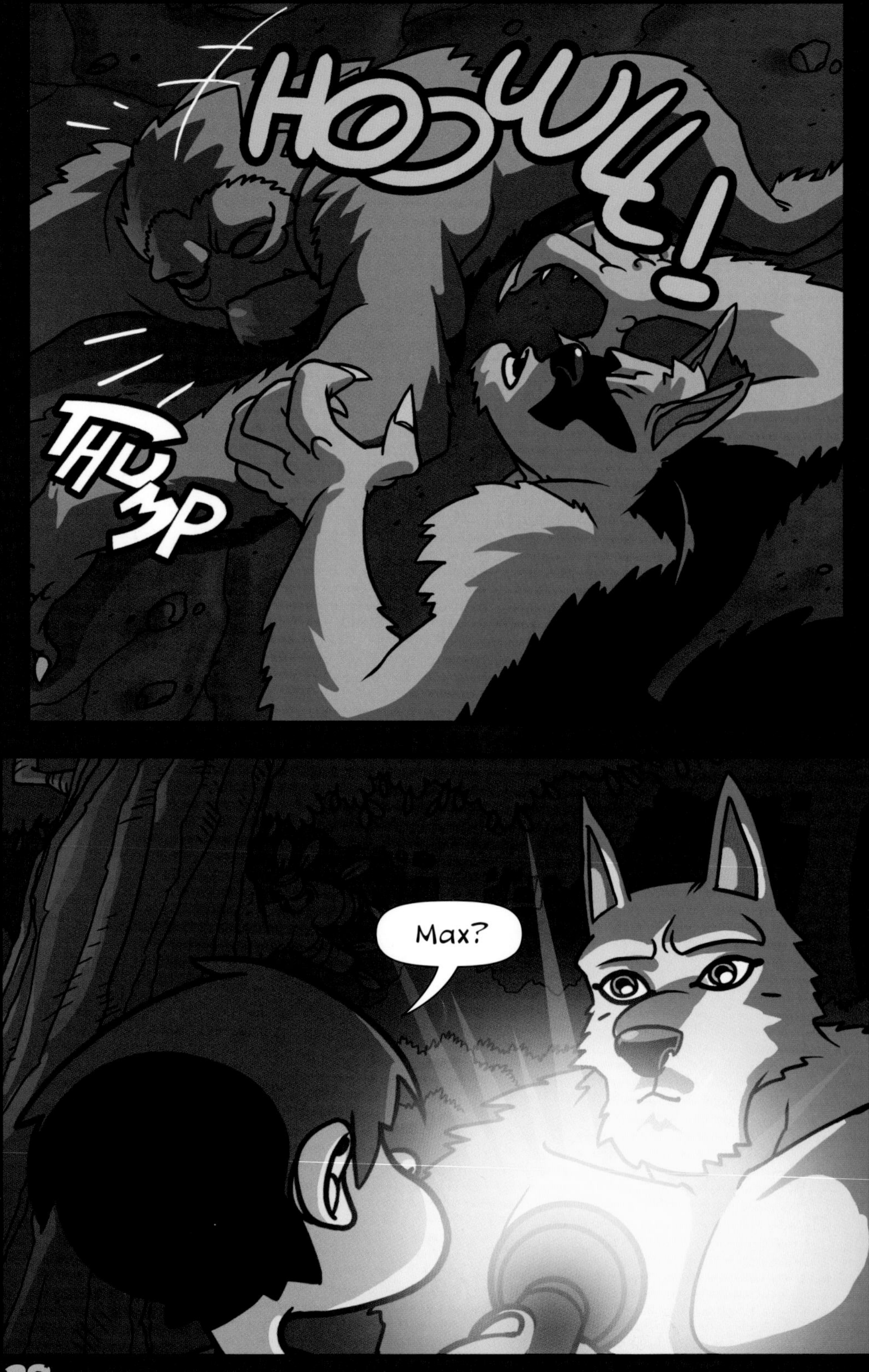
HOOWL!
THUMP
Max?

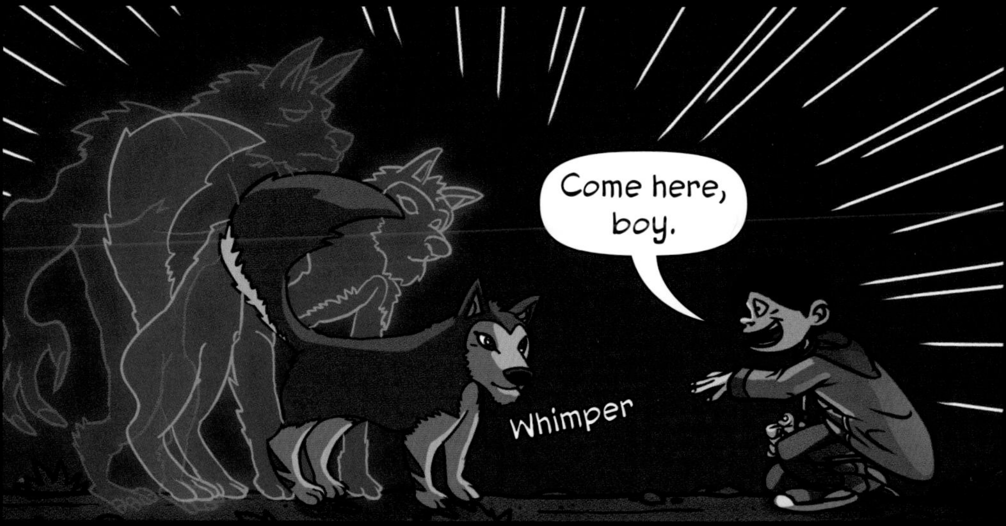
Come here, boy.
Whimper

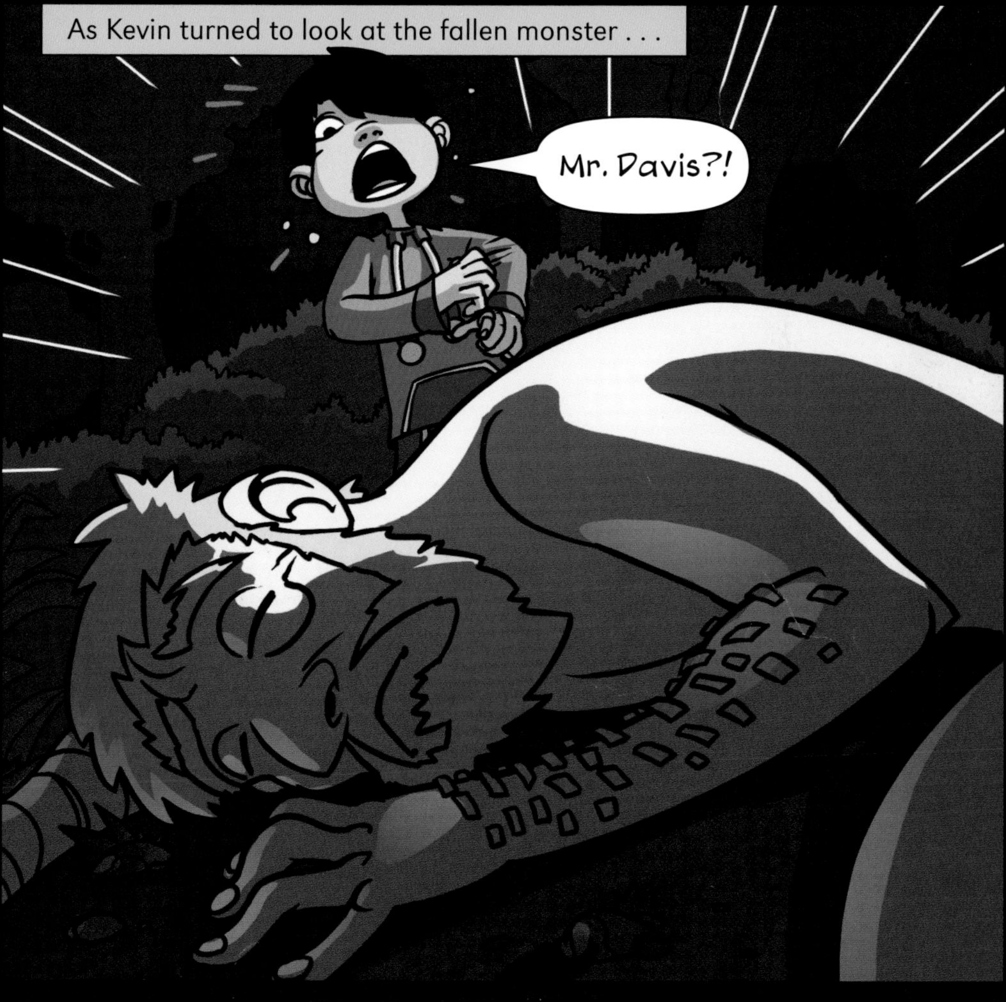
As Kevin turned to look at the fallen monster . . .
Mr. Davis?!

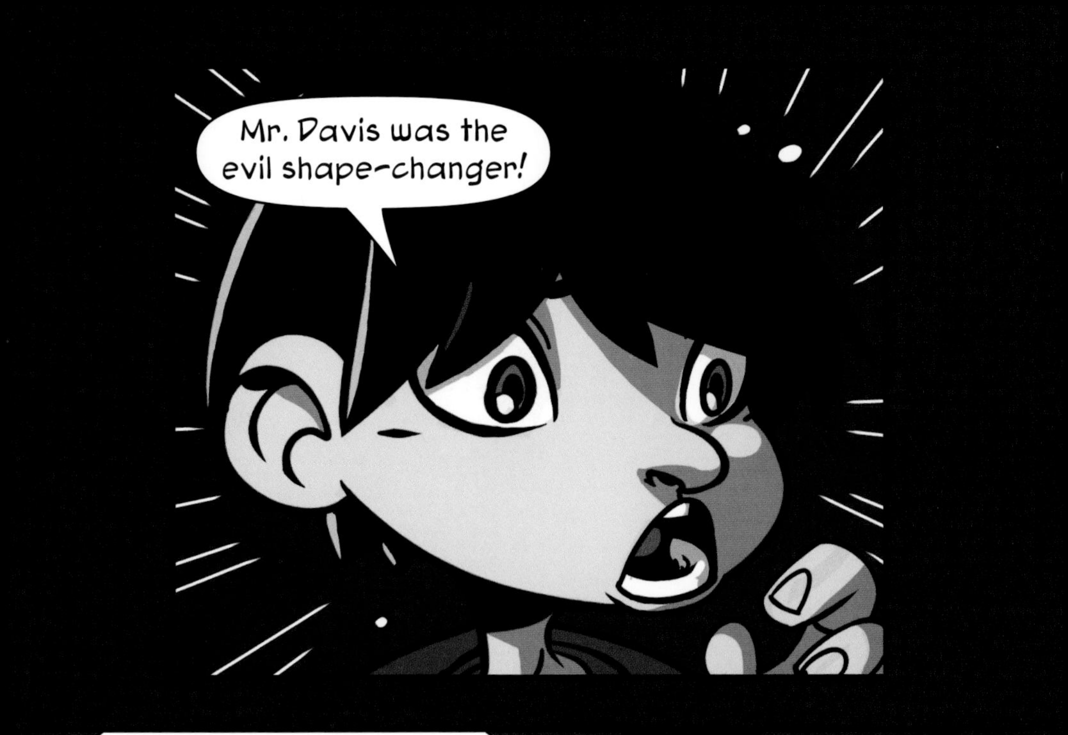
Mr. Davis was the evil shape-changer!

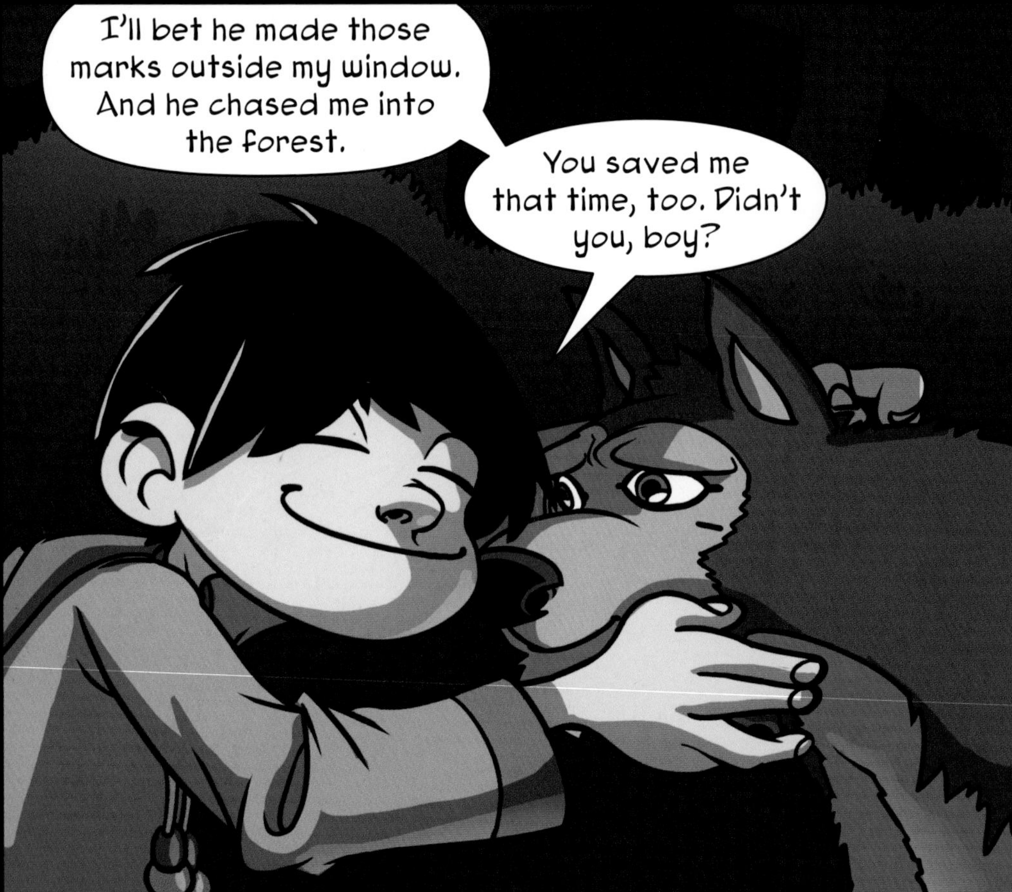
I'll bet he made those marks outside my window. And he chased me into the forest.
You saved me that time, too. Didn't you, boy?

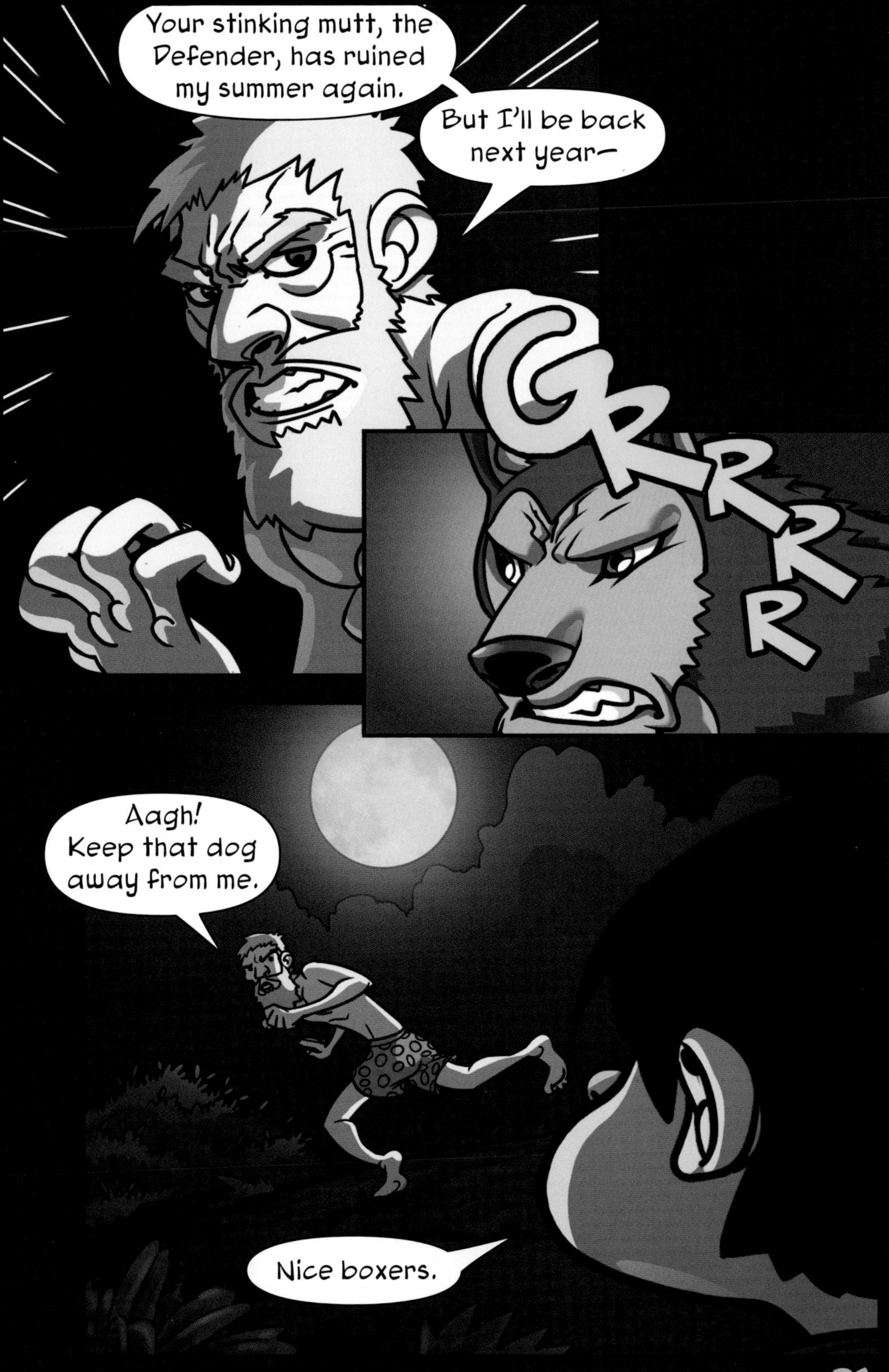

Your stinking mutt, the Defender, has ruined my summer again.
But I'll be back next year—
GRRRR
Aagh! Keep that dog away from me.
Nice boxers.

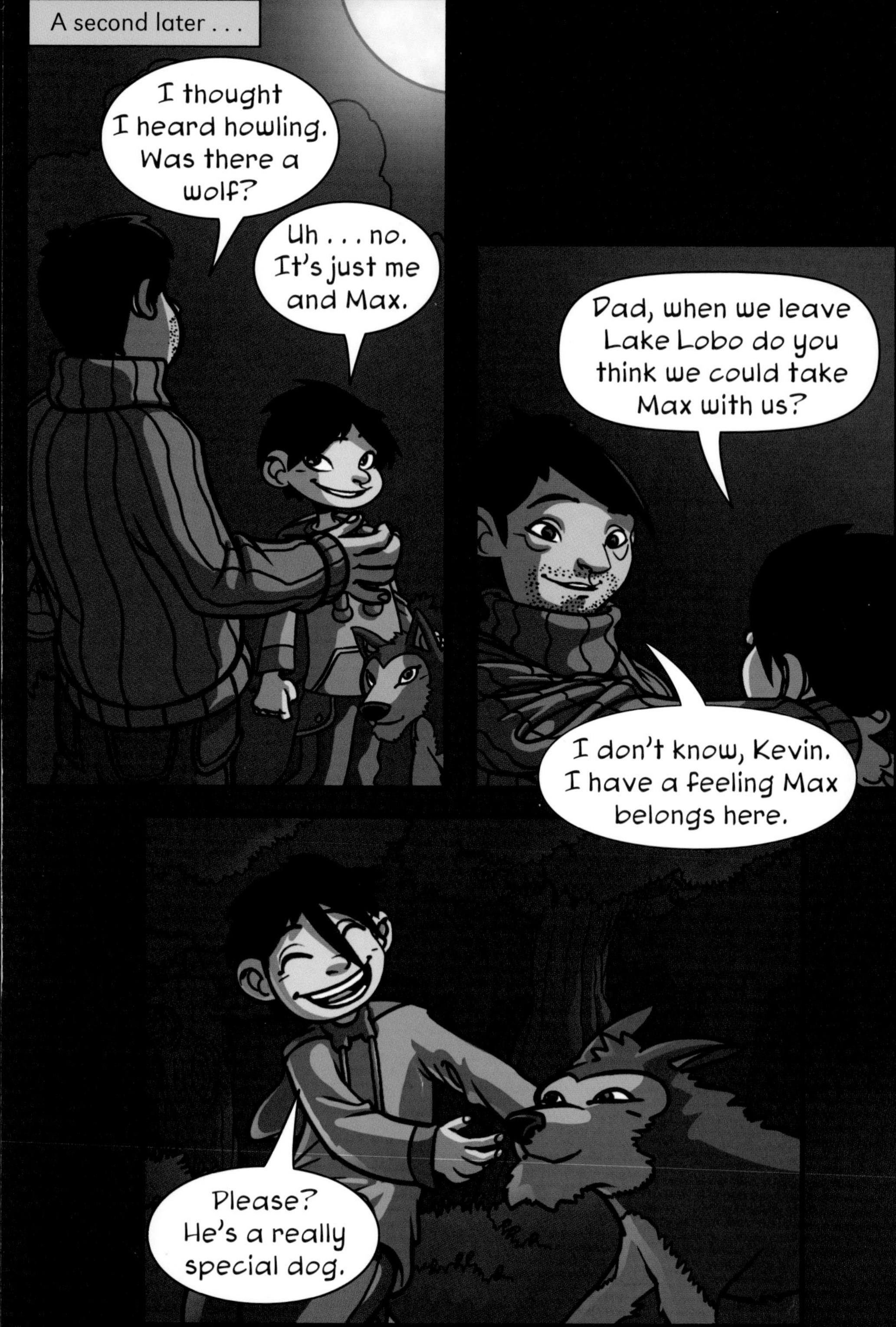
A second later . . .
I thought I heard howling. Was there a wolf?
Uh . . . no. It's just me and Max.
Dad, when we leave Lake Lobo do you think we could take Max with us?
I don't know, Kevin. I have a feeling Max belongs here.
Please? He's a really special dog.

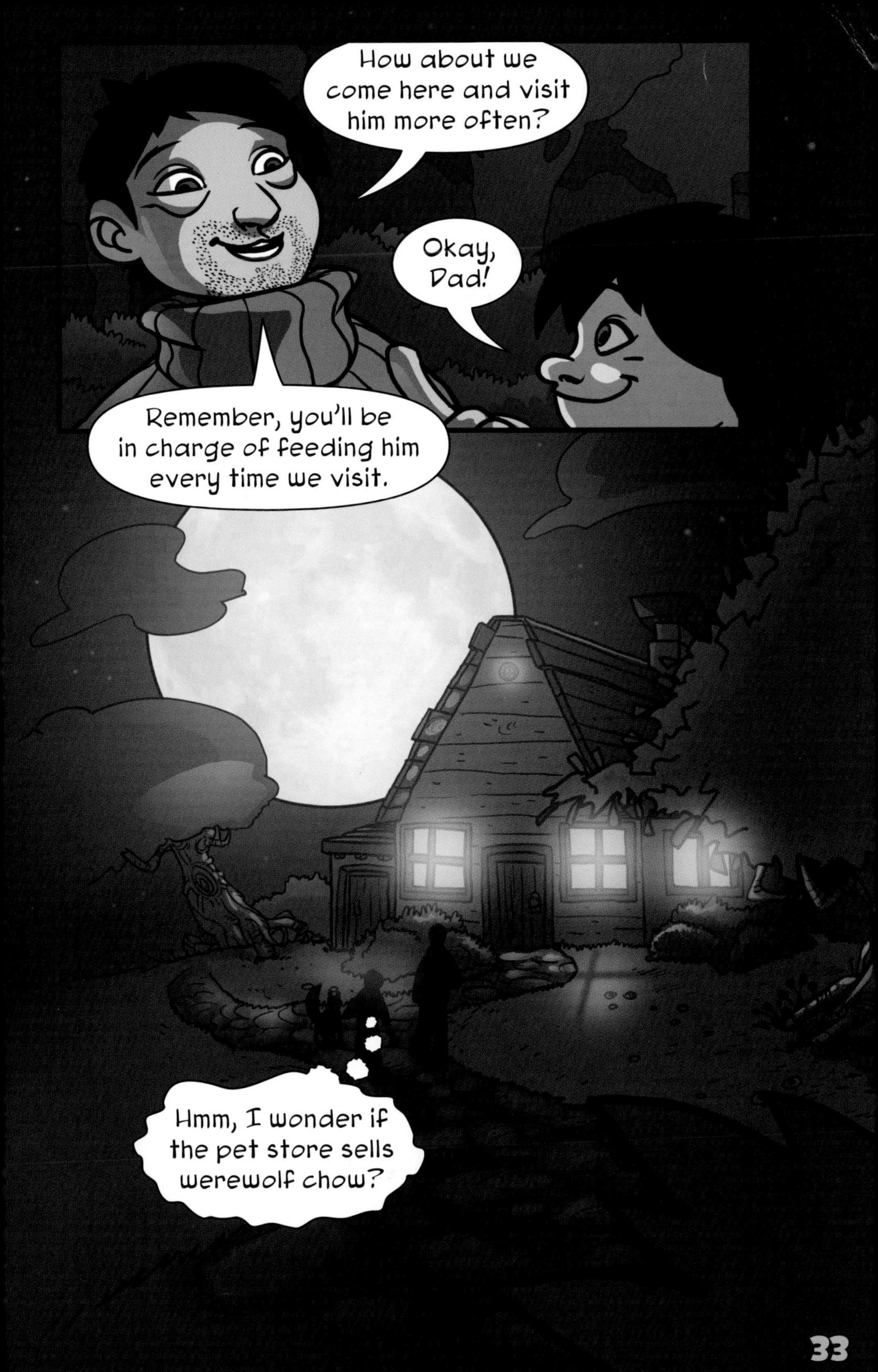
How about we come here and visit him more often?
Okay, Dad!
Remember, you'll be in charge of feeding him every time we visit.
Hmm, I wonder if the pet store sells werewolf chow?

ABOUT THE AUTHOR

Born in 1962 in Denver, Colorado, Scott Nickel works by day at Paws, Inc., Jim Davis's famous Garfield studio, and he freelances by night. Burning the midnight oil, Scott has created hundreds of humorous greeting cards and written several children's books, short fiction for *Boys' Life* magazine, comic strips, and lots of really funny knock-knock jokes. He was raised in Southern California, but in 1995 Scott moved to Indiana, where he currently lives with his wife, two sons, six cats, and several sea monkeys.

ABOUT THE ILLUSTRATOR

Enrique (ehn-REE-kay) Corts became a professional illustrator at age 19, working on short stories for a Spanish comic magazine. After finishing his art studies, he entered the graphic design and advertising world, spending endless hours chained to his computer. Later, he worked as a concept artist in Great Britain on video games such as *Worms 3D, EyeToy Play 3,* and *Play 4.*

Enrique currently lives in Palma de Mallorca, Spain, with his girlfriend Mar. Enrique thinks perhaps someday he will go back to his native Valencia in his quest for more sunlight.

GLOSSARY

caretaker (KAIR-tay-kuhr)—a person who takes care of a building or another person; not all caretakers are evil shape-changers.

chow (CHAU)—food, grub, good stuff to eat. Not to be confused with **chow chow**, which is a kind of dog. Or with **chow chow chow**, which is a kind of dog food.

defender (di-FEN-duhr)—a protector or guardian. Lake Lobo is watched over by a special defender.

lobo (LOH-boh)—the Spanish word for "wolf"

shape-changer (SHAYP-chayn-juhr)—a creature that can turn into something else. Werewolves are shape-changers.

werewolf (WAIR-wulf)—a person or animal that can change into a wolf

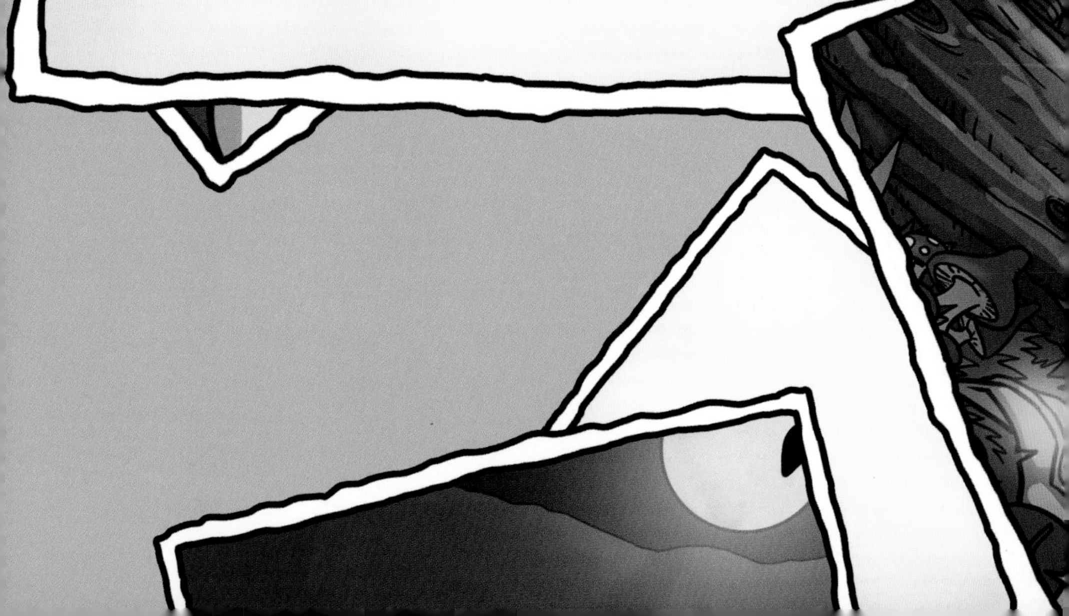

FACTS TO HOWL ABOUT

Dogs are part of the family called *Canidae (KAN-uh-dee)*. This animal family also includes coyotes, jackals, foxes, and wolves.

All pet dogs are descended from gray wolves. About 12,000 years ago, these types of wolves started hanging around people. Eventually, the humans began using them for hunting, herding, and as pets.

Today, the American Kennel Club recognizes 155 different breeds of dogs. Since 1991, the most popular dog in the United States has been the Labrador retriever.

Many wolves and dogs still look alike. In fact, adult dogs and wolves have the same number of teeth. They both have 20 teeth on the top and 22 teeth on the bottom.

Both dogs and wolves like to howl but not at the full moon. They actually howl to warn off enemies or to find friends in the distance.

How did Max know that Mr. Davis was the Monster of Lake Lobo? Maybe he used his super sniffer. Dogs and wolves have ultra-sensitive noses. They can smell 100 times better than humans.

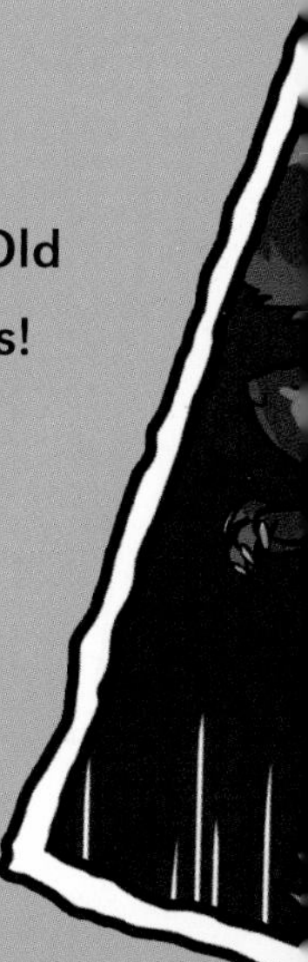

Many experts believe the largest dog on record was an Old English mastiff named Zorba, which weighed 343 pounds! The smallest dog was a teeny tiny Yorkie, which weighed only 4 ounces.

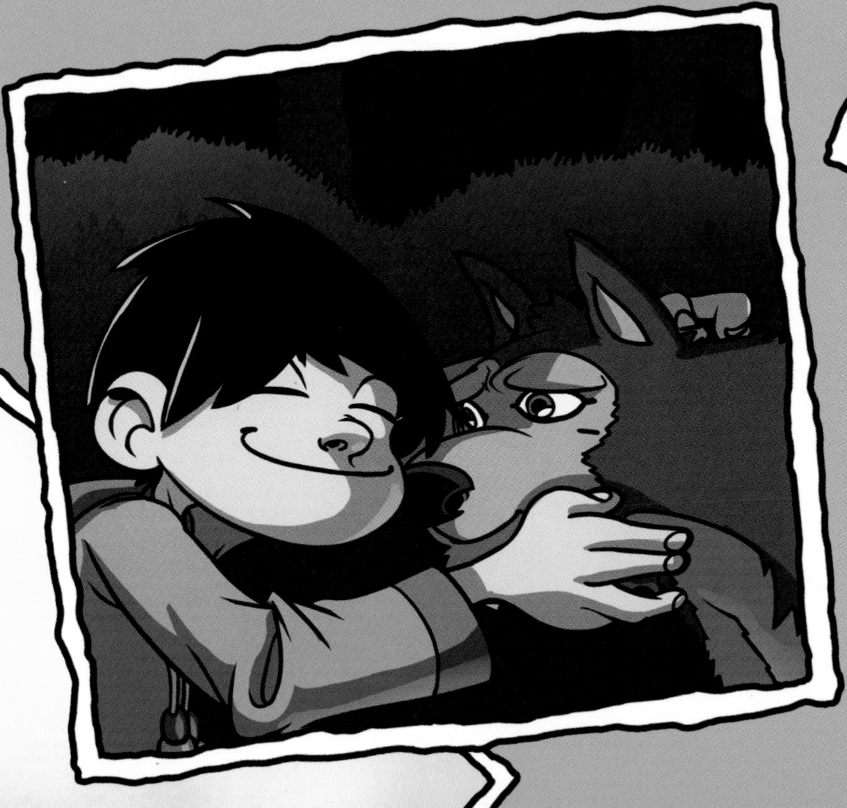

DISCUSSION QUESTIONS

1.) Do you think Kevin should have known that Mr. Davis was the evil shape-changer? What were some of the clues?

2.) Mr. Davis, the evil shape-changer, scares people because he wants the lake for himself. Do you ever want to be alone? Since you can't turn into a monster, how do you get privacy?

3.) At the end of the story, Kevin's dad puts him in charge of feeding Max. Have you ever been responsible for an important job? What was the job and how did you get it done?

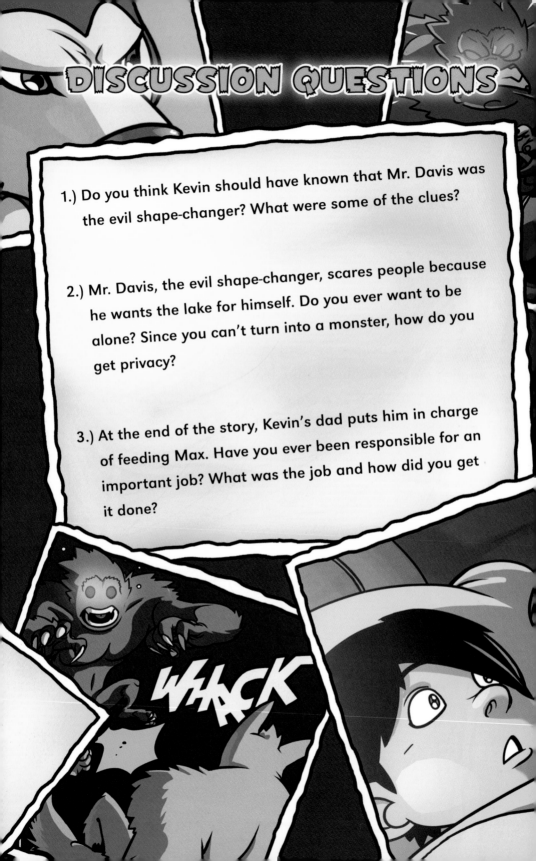

WRITING PROMPTS

1.) Kevin's summer vacation at Lake Lobo turns into a pretty crazy trip. Write about your best summer vacation. What made the trip fun or even crazy?

2.) A legend is a story that's been told by many people for many years. Think of a story that someone told you, and write it down. Then, read or pass along the story to someone else.

3.) In the story, both Max and Mr. Davis are shape-changers and can turn into something else. If you were a shape-changer, what would you become? Describe what you would do as something else.

INTERNET SITES

Do you want to know more about subjects related to this book? Or are you interested in learning about other topics? Then check out FactHound, a fun, easy way to find Internet sites.

Our investigative staff has already sniffed out great sites for you!

Here's how to use FactHound:

1. Visit *www.facthound.com*

2. Select your grade level.

3. To learn more about subjects related to this book, type in the book's ISBN number: **1598898361**.

4. Click the **Fetch It** button.

FactHound will fetch the best Internet sites for you!